american

sorrows

D1738782

american sorrows

sorrows

jay

lake

american sorrows

Published by

Wheatland Press

http://www.wheatlandpress.com
P. O. Box 1818
Wilsonville, OR 97070

Library of Congress Cataloging-in-Publication data is available upon request.
ISBN 0-9755903-0-8
Printed in the United States of America
Cover photograph by Aynjel Kaye.

Wheatland Press

http://www.wheatlandpress.com

There are more people to thank in this year of my life than
I could ever put names to on this page,
so this one's for Bronwyn.
The rest of you know I love you, too.

introduction

Aficionados of fantasy genre literature have been discussing lately what the trends are. Have we entered the world of the "new weird"? Has "slipstream" replaced the older traditions? Has the word itself, "genre," lost its meaning?

Whatever the case is, you can be sure that when a writer sits down with pen and paper (or word processor), that literary discussions of today's movements drop away. They become moot. What matters most after a few minutes in that special reverie which is the writer's own, is the story. And among storytellers, there's a select group who not only have a story to tell, but also have a compelling voice to grab you by the ears and make you pay attention. "Something vital is going on here," it will say. "Something that will move you and entertain you and leave you thinking."

That's a Jay Lake kind of storyteller.

In this collection you will find four assuredly told stories by Jay Lake, who both has the confidence in his own tales to plunge in without hesitation, and faith in the readers to follow him. These stories take us immediately into real worlds not quite like our own, but so unerringly told that you'll be asking yourself if maybe, just maybe, they aren't fantastic at all.

In "Our Lady of American Sorrows," a parallel history to ours plunges us deep into political intrigue, high adventure and Mayan mysticism. While I was reading, though, I found myself wondering if the events of that world weren't real. Did I miss a day in my history class? Did the Pope really have access to nuclear weaponry? What *were* the effects of the second great war on South American politics? I don't know, and in that area of ignorance, Jay has woven his story.

The setting of "The River Knows Its Own" is a Portland I recognize, complete with achingly funny caricatures of grunge environmentalists and the fringe folks who practice environmentalism like it's a black magic, except in Jay's world, the magic works. The story never ceases to be a dead-on portrait of one segment of our society, and all the while it isn't about our world at all, at least not the part of it you will be familiar with.

Clearly the Texas of "Into the Gardens of Sweet Night" isn't ours, but everything within it is, warped and twisted and familiar, even the talking pug and the very purposeful wolves. In this, my favorite story in the collection, Jay takes us on a ride that is reminiscent of pulp fiction at its best. A rollicking adventure filled with surprises. Readers had best hold onto their wits while reading this one.

"Daddy's Caliban" is the only piece here that doesn't seem firmly grounded in a place you'll recognize, at least not recognize like you would Portland, Texas or New Albion, Oregon, America's west coast, but it's a place you'll recognize emotionally. This is a child's world told from a young person's sensibility. It's a world of brothers playing together, investigating river currents and the mystery of adults.

But where I think Jay excels best as a storyteller is that he has a love of things. Sandra McPhearson, a poet I admire, once said that a poem can be judged by its "thing count." If you consider a poem as an envelope, how many things does it have in it? Can you open the envelope and shake a pile of things out? If you can't, then the poem might be lacking. Stories can be considered that way too. Jay's stories are filled with things to see, touch, taste, smell and hear. There are elusive green parrots and *Panthera tigris sumatrae* and dirigibles and ragged dragons, and a host of other solid, concrete persons, places and, well, things.

Jay is a thoughtful and articulate person. I've heard him expound on writing theory with the best of them. He knows his way around the academic version of the writers' world, where sometimes it seems that writers don't consider themselves to be successful unless they are writing a work that only the smartest five-hundred people in the world can appreciate. Jay's stories aren't like that. They're informed by his profound thinking about language and narrative, but they are always stories first.

If this book is your introduction to the work of Jay Lake, and it leaves you wanting more, rest assured that there is a lot of it out there. Jay has been writing up a storm. Reading a Jay Lake story is like settling in around the campfire. The wood crackles cheerfully; the smoke curls pleasantly into the forest around you; the stars glitter with that special hard edge that mountain air provides, and just when you are comfortable, Jay joins you at the edge of light. "I have a story to tell," he says.

And he does.

James Van Pelt
July, 2004

contents

our lady of american sorrows

I sat with my friend Rodger—two months older and taller than me, but otherwise close as any twin brother—on the flat stone roof of my family's house, second from the end of the row on the steepest block of Rondo Street. We were both sixteen, and this was our last summer of freedom before our final year at Latin School, before we had to work for our livings. The day was so hot it felt as if the sun itself reached down to press on my head.

We shared our perch with a handful of iguanas and a pair of dusty-winged crows. We could see half the town, from the landing field along the river to east, back to the Civil Palace downtown. A series of open-topped trucks belched black smoke as they strained up the cobbles of Charles Avenue, coming from Ostia, New Albion's little port at the river's mouth. Four in three hours!

Each was filled with straight-backed men in black cassocks, their dog collars visible like white slashes against their throats even from our distance. They all were heading for the monastery west of town—Our Lady of American Sorrows, a great fortress of a holy house inhabited only by solemn Cistercians.

Until now. I sincerely doubted these were more Cistercian brothers come to call. "Four trucks," I said. "Perhaps a dozen priests in each."

Rodger snickered. "Are there enough souls in danger here in New Albion to need fifty new priests?"

"No one needs fifty new priests," I said darkly.

Papa was a theist, which was legal in New Albion, sort of. Even though Mama had raised me well I found his skepticism daring. Last Sunday at Mass at St. Cipriano's, Father Lavigne told us that Pope Louis-Charles III had sworn a renewed mission in the Americas when he had elevated the

1

Archbishop of Teixeira. But *fifty* priests? If the Holy Office were coming to test the faith of our parishes, Papa would be in trouble.

I tried to imagine another reason for the priests to be here, hoping to conjure some little word-magic to offset my newfound fear. "Perhaps they are headed for the interior, to the native countries."

Rodger's snort was answer enough for that. "Just you watch," he said. "Something big is brewing."

No more trucks appeared, and the next aeroplane wasn't due until Friday, so after a while we got our fly rods and crickets to go fishing for bats off the seaside cliffs at sundown. The catch was always difficult, but they crisped so well on the fire, and tasted delicious with sea salt, lime and ground peppers.

New Albion sprawls across dusty hills that are almost never hidden from the sun. Despite what they say about us in Avignon and Londres, it does rain here, at least at certain hours of the day during certain times of the year. Our little country is known mostly for our heat and our cloudless summers, and beaches which stretch at the feet of pale cliffs two hours' walk to the east.

We were also known, I suppose, for our coffee. That plant grows in abundance, both wild and cultivated, in the high hills far to the west of town, where there is shade and rain drifts down from the distant mountains. Somehow God arranged it so we had neither ocean nor coffee ourselves here in New Albion proper, but were rather simply caught in the middle ground between the salt spray and the morning's benediction.

Papa had been working on a new kind of coffee mill ever since I could remember. He had a job as well, at the Ministry of Commercial Affairs in a high-windowed office down by the sluggish river that he sometimes took me to see. He sat under an old wicker-bladed fan that squealed in a slow tempo, stamping seals on forms after holding them in files for long periods of time. Since his mother was Brasilian, it was good that Papa had a civil service job—anyone with Brasilian connections had been under suspicion since the Second Great War.

Another reason to fear the new priests.

Papa went down to his office three or four days a week, stamped papers for a while, then counted the circling flies until the sweat beneath his collar drove him home again. The rest of the time he labored in the little workshop across the alley behind our block of whitewashed houses. Undershirt grimy with oil, Gauloise dangling from his lips, Papa sent sparks showering from his welder or patiently rewound electric motors. Somehow the heat did not bother Papa so much when he worked on his own projects.

There were two very old coffee mills built into the slope of the hillside just south of Papa's workshop, where the alley rises higher. Each was as big as a small house, with a door into the lower level. They still had mule troughs alongside their loading platforms, and hand pumps to bring the water up to the separator tanks. Both were overhung by enormous banyan trees.

The mills always looked to me like kilns, great squat shapes with their tanks and pipes and chutes and gears. One even had the original wood-fired boiler still attached, which once had driven the pulping press, though it had long been reduced to a still for mash fermented from durians and coconuts gathered along our quiet beaches. The electric wires tied off to the banyan trees sparked in thunderstorms, but still the mills always worked when the grinding-men came to start them up in coffee season.

Papa sometimes stood before them at dusk, once he had lost the light in his workshop. He smoked, staring at the limestone walls and the teakwood separator tanks as if they, not the stunning heat or New Albion's aching bureaucracy, were his true enemy. "Listen to me, Peter João Fallworth," he had said more than once, stabbing the cigarette like a tiny orange comet in the dusk. "You are almost a man. Understand this: it is the coffee that keeps us poor. The factors from the commodities bourses in São Paulo and Londres own us through those damned beans as much as any plantation overseer of the last century." Flick, the Gauloise blazed away to the center of the alley, far from the dry brush. Only its sharp scent remained, the smoke lingering like our pale dust always does.

"Slaves," he would say. "We are as slaves."

I never could understand why Papa's coffee mill was better than the old mills, or how it was supposed to free us. Though Mama hated it, he liked to talk about political economy and natural rights over our corn and turkey stews, but New Albion was already free. There hadn't been slaves here for almost a hundred years, and they'd almost all gone to Brasil when they were manumitted. Father Lavigne preached liberation on Sundays, and my teachers at the Latin School said the same during the week.

Me, I was my own person only on Saturdays, except during the summers when I was free as any ex-slave. Even that was almost over, as next year would be my last at the Latin School.

On Wednesday Rodger and I were down in the free market, spending our few hard-earned Albion pounds on fried pies and shopping for rumors of the new priests. I wanted to know if they were Jesuits, who often worked for the Holy Office. We heard a rumbling in the sky above us that drowned out even the bleating of the goats in their pens.

We both looked up.

"That's a *jet*," Rodger said in an awed voice. Every month or so through the post he got an aviation magazine from Nouveau Orleans. It wasn't really a proper magazine, more of a fly-specked thing folded down from a large sheet that was printed in French he could barely read, but it continually fueled his passion for flight. Aeroplanes were one of the few areas of life where I would admit to his superior wisdom without argument. "Look..." He used his half-eaten pie to point, jabbing me in the ribs with his free hand. "See, no propellers."

The aeroplane was too *big* to be up in the air like that. Despite myself, I felt a tiny shiver of fear. "Where are the engines? How does it stay up?"

"The *wings* keep it up, dummy." His tone would have withered bananas. "That's where the engines are, too. See how fat the wings are close to the body? That's why it's a *jet*."

We both stared. The usual aeroplane from Teixeira was short and fat, with a huge propeller engine in each wing. Rodger called it a gooneybird, and said it was a veteran of the Second Great War. This jet aeroplane was long and silver, like a flying cigarillo wrapped in foil. The tail was red, with the Papal key in gold, and a French tricolor on the top of the rudder. It roared like a jaguar, where the usual aeroplane whined like an enormous wasp.

"Do you suppose it flew straight here from Avignon?" I asked.

He snickered. "The Comète doesn't have that kind of range. It probably flew to Bermuda, then down to Spanish Florida. San Agustin or that big Armée de l'Aire base at Santa Lucia, I'd guess. From there it would be an easy hop across the Caribbean."

"But why?" There was no aeroplane due today. It must have something to do with the priests.

The jet made another pass over the city. That was the usual signal for the pilots from Teixeira to have the Civil Guard clear the landing field down by the river of stray cattle or football games or whatever other uses the shantytown people had got up to for the wide open space.

Business in the market had come to a halt as people stood and stared, chattering or keeping an awed silence depending on their character. It was clear very few of them had Rodger's information.

"Come on," I said, "let's get down to the landing field."

We trotted toward the market gates and Water Avenue beyond even as a distant bell began to ring. The deep tone could only be the Grand Bell at Our Lady of American Sorrows west of town. As Rodger and I made our way down the street St. Cipriano's bells picked up the ringing, followed by Santa Clara and the tinny ones at All Angels', and the bells further east that I didn't recognize by ear.

"Can you tell me why the bells are ringing?" shouted a red-faced fat woman from her doorstep, an enameled pan of beans trembling in her hands.

We both shrugged. "Perhaps the Pope has come!" called Rodger. Despite myself, I laughed as we began to run.

Then the carillon at the Civil Palace picked up the peal, and the sirens of the Civil Guard wailed as their jitneys poured into the street, and then it wasn't so much fun any more. Rodger and I scuttled into a little café and pretended to look at stale pastries in the fly-specked case until the jitneys had roared past. The proprietor said nothing, just kept reading his newspaper with one eye on us in case of theft.

Though the minions of New Albion's government rarely stirred themselves to action, everyone knew to practice prudence when they did. That Papa was one of 'them' had never occurred to me before today, but I stared at the crumbling currant scones, suddenly ashamed of who I was.

Rodger and I picked our way along the riverbank toward the landing field, stones in hand to drive off the shantytown kids if they hassled us. They were far more dangerous than the occasional alligator come too far up the river. Today though, the arrival of the jet and the Civil Guard scrambling in the streets was more interesting than a couple of boys strayed down from the hills.

The shanties didn't quite come to the water. Rather, they stopped at the muddy bluff overlooking the river, just about the high water mark during rainy season. Right now in summer there were dosses and firepits all over the stony beach, where people slept out under the stars to catch the breeze and a few dozen extra mosquito bites. Their houses were built from big steel shipping containers, or coffee crates patched together, or just plain old scrap wood and deadfall. There were even a few made from decrepit busses retired from the overland express routes. No two were alike, except for the little plumes of smoke from their cooking fires and the pervasive odor of rancid corn oil. Mangy dogs growled from doorways while wild-eyed cats ran feral among brown-skinned toddlers playing in the dirt.

Whenever I complained that we were poor, in our whitewashed house high up on Rondo Street, Mama would send me down to the center of New Albion on some errand near the river, making sure I walked by this place. When I got home again, I would sink to my knees beside my bed and thank God for what wealth we had.

There was a spit of land ahead of us, mud and sand caught up behind a tall rock everyone called the Bishop's Head. If you were polite, or too young to understand, you said it was because it looked like a man wearing a churchman's miter. There was a tangle of trees on the spit, which meant we either had to climb the bluff to our right and actually walk *through* the shantytown, or we had to pick our way along the stones in the water on the other side of the Bishop's Head. In rainy season, that would be near-suicidal, but in summer, there was little risk of anything beyond damp feet.

Rodger said nothing, and neither did I. We both cut left, following the water's edge. The stones rolled beneath our shoes, cheap canvas sneakers from the factories of Spanish Florida, but we kept our balance. I was slightly in front of Rodger when I got to the Bishop's Head itself.

I had one hand on the stone, balancing against the warm, gritty surface as I watched my feet carefully. There were a couple of pools deep enough to soak me to the thighs there, and always the possibility of turning an ankle. I almost stepped on a black cloth floating in the water, overbalancing to avoid it, when I realized it was man.

"Ahh!" I shouted, then shut up.

Rodger almost ran into me. "What is—" he started to snap, then stopped as he saw it too.

It wasn't just a man, it was a priest. Face down in the river. With a ragged, bloody hole in the back of his head.

My stomach heaved, and I vomited, trying to lean away from the dead man.

"They will kill us," Rodger said quietly when I was done. "Just for knowing of this."

"It has to be the new priests," I said. I was shivering, and my nose stung. I cupped my hand and reached down for some water to wash my mouth out, then stopped. I did not want to drink of this priest's death. I finished my thought. "The water's always deep up by Our Lady of American Sorrows, but no one from New Albion would expect this river to carry a body away in summertime."

"Priests." Rodger made the word a curse. "Killing is a sin. I am quite sure it says so in *my* Bible."

Reaching down, I touched the dead man's shoulder. He bobbed in his little pool.

"Don't," Rodger said.

"I have to." I realized we were whispering now. I stepped in with the corpse and pushed down harder, then caught his other shoulder and turned him.

I recognized the man. It was a brother from Our Lady of American Sorrows who had occasionally assisted with Mass at St. Cipriano's. It made me sad that I did not know his name. He still wore his hand-carved pectoral cross over his cassock, and a look of sad surprise on his gray-fleshed face. I tried to close his eyes, which were clouded and dull, but the open lids were wrinkled tight from the water.

Instead I took his hand. A priest probably needed no help from me to get into Heaven, but I was pretty sure no one had given him last rites. I couldn't do that either, but I could pray for him.

After a few moments, we headed back the way we had come. "Why?" Rodger asked after a time, but I had no answer.

At home, Mama glared at my muddy pants and wrinkled sneakers. "Where have you been?" she demanded. "Swimming in that filthy river?"

"Please, Mama, not now." I wanted to tell her what I had seen, hand the problem of the dead priest to someone older and wiser, but Mama would just be afraid and run to Father Lavigne. Papa would know what to do, but he was downtown in his high-windowed office, or perhaps out at the landing field with whoever the Pope had sent to trouble us.

I felt a burst of guilty relief that whatever troubles had come to town were not about my father. The Holy Office would not have shot a priest to dump him in the river. But they were still troubles, terrible troubles, even if the Holy Office were not involved.

I could certainly run to Father Lavigne myself, but I was worried. For him, for me, for New Albion. These truckloads of priests were poison for us all.

"Mrs. Dalhousie says that new aeroplane brought a cardinal all the way from Avignon," Mama said. "He must be here to consecrate the mission of those new priests." She leaned close. "I worry about them."

It was as if she had read my mind. I thought when I got older that sort of thing would stop. "Me too, Mama."

"Mrs. Dalhousie says they're *Jesuits*." She looked around, as if one were hiding behind the door of our kitchen. "Big men."

Watching with Rodger, I had only seen them in the backs of the trucks. It was hard to tell how big they really were.

Big enough to kill our local priests, I realized.

"I don't know, Mama," I said. "Can I go change my clothes?"

She ruffled my hair and smiled, beauty passing across her face like a momentary shadow. "Yes, Peter, you *may* change. Go wash up, too." Mama raised her voice. "And Rodger, you may come in from the alley and have a cup of tea."

"I'm a mess, Mrs. Fallworth," he said from the alley.

"So is my floor, thanks to Peter. I'll set out a pan for you to wash your shoes."

I went to our little bathroom and scrubbed until I couldn't feel the rough dampness of the dead priest's cassock on my hands anymore.

That afternoon, Rodger and I got our rods, some salt and ground peppers, a wicker cricket case and two old bananas for bug bait. "We're fishing for bats," I told Mama.

"I don't want you out late," she said. "Not with all these goings on."

"We'll be safe at the coast. No one ever goes there." Which was more or less true, except for tourists and the people who worked in Ostia. "We might even sleep out."

She kissed me, which she hadn't done so much these last few years. "Come back safe," Mama said, then we stepped out into the alley.

"We're not going to the coast," said Rodger.

"No way." I shivered, the image of the dead man in the river very clear in my head. "I want to get a better look at these new priests."

"Good," he said. "You're smarter than you seem."

We stashed our gear in the pressing room of one of the old coffee mills and headed up the alley to be out of sight if Mama stepped out the back door. Once we made it to Formby Way, the next cross street, we headed west.

Our Lady of American Sorrows is on Bullback Hill. The road out there is a westward extension of Water Avenue into the countryside that finally leaves the riverbank and switchbacks up to the monastery. The back wall hangs forty meters or more up above the river at a wide bend, which was where the dead priest must have been shot and thrown off before floating down to the Bishop's Head. But there was an old sacbe, a Mayan road, that ran westward parallel to the river just behind a line of bluffs, coming quite close to the monastery without being visible from it.

I figured the new priests wouldn't know about the sacbe yet, since no one used it but goatherds. The Cistercian brothers weren't likely saying much right now.

As we walked past the Catalpa Street Oil Depot, a government jitney drove by. Brakes screeched as it slammed to a halt just in front of us. Rodger and I looked at each other, but there wasn't much point in running.

Yet.

Then Papa got out.

My heart sank. He had a revolver on his belt. I had never seen him carry a weapon in my entire life, not so much as a machete. He looked very angry, but judging from the way his eyes darted around, not at me.

"Are you crazy, Peter," Papa hissed. "This is no time to be on the streets!"

"I..." I wanted to tell him about the dead priest, ask him what to do, but

I couldn't see who was driving the jitney. Papa had gotten out of the left side, the passenger side. I wasn't afraid of him, but I was afraid of what his job might make him do.

Papa cleared his throat. "You boys go home," he almost shouted. His voice had a weird, false heartiness. He was lying at the top of his lungs. His eyes kept darting to the left, his head almost shivering.

"Yes, sir," Rodger suddenly shouted back, and grabbed my elbow. "Right away."

Papa jerked his chin left, set one hand on his pistol, and bellowed, "Get out of here, then!"

We got. Rodger almost dragged me away from my own father, into the nearest alley. Papa jumped back in his jitney, which took off with a squeal of tires. Immediately afterward we heard a diesel straining up the hill.

Rodger and I peeked out.

It was another open-topped truck, like the ones we had seen carrying the priests yesterday. There was a machine gun mounted on a pintle just behind the cab. Half a dozen Civil Guardsmen sat in back with rifles pointing over the side.

"It's a coup," Rodger said.

"Against *what*? New Albion barely *has* a government."

The last alcaldé had died of cholera when I was twelve. In the four years since, New Albion had simply kept functioning under a ministerial junta. I'd learned in school that our little country was technically an English protectorate, but there had been no financial or political support from Londres for several generations. In practice, when high justice was required or something irresolvable happened in government, the abbot from Our Lady of American Sorrows was consulted, or a message sent to the archbishop in Teixeira.

As Papa liked to say, the death of the alcaldé simply streamlined that process.

"Maybe there will be a new alcaldé," Rodger said.

"Like we need one."

We heard a popping noise from downhill, toward the middle of the city. Sirens wailed.

"Guns?" I asked, just as the unmistakable stutter of a machine gun began.

Rodger and I hid among the pipes of the oil depot until dusk, long after the gunfire and the screams had died away, though the open-topped trucks continued to rumble through the streets of town.

Evening found us picking our way along the goat paths among the hills. We caught occasional glimpses of Our Lady of American Sorrows, the monastery's walls floodlit as if for a festival. Someone was taking no chances. But whom? With what?

The paths were winding dirt tracks among the stubbly scrub of the hillsides. Once, so I had been told, there had been great forests along this coast, but centuries of logging and farming had driven them back and dried out the soil. At least it was not so dusty here.

Walking single file, Rodger and I had little to say to one another. I kept thinking of Papa's gun, and the truck that had followed him. Had those men been under his orders? Had any of the shots been fired by him?

Some concern of the world had come to New Albion, something larger than coffee or tourism or our notion of civil affairs.

"Peter." Right in front of me, Rodger stopped. His voice was a whisper.

I stopped too, snapped out of my thoughts and looked around. Two or three hundred meters ahead, in a copse of bushes where the sacbe first assembled itself from scattered gravel, a gleaming spark rose and fell. For a moment, I thought a star had come to earth, a sign to accompany the Papal jet that had landed that afternoon.

"Sentry," Rodger breathed.

Then I realized that what I had seen was a match, someone lighting a cigarette. Like Papa in front of the old mills at home.

By unspoken agreement we both worked our way up the bank to our right until we could look over the crest. Just like playing Great War when we were younger, shooting each other with sticks and throwing cowpie grenadoes.

The monastery still gleamed, its floodlights making the high, smooth walls seem marble instead of limestone. Though we were several kilometers from it, the clatter of the diesel generator echoed across the distance. The river beyond the monastery, visible where it appeared from behind Bullback Hill, gleamed in the rising moon.

No sign of sentries. No one pacing the walls of Our Lady of American

Sorrows. No trucks or guards on the road that wound up the hill to the gates.

"Why is someone up here?" I finally asked. "They can't know about the sacbe."

"I don't know." Rodger sounded puzzled.

"They were shooting people in town today."

"Not *them*."

I could hear the rustle as he nodded toward the monastery. Rodger was thinking of Papa, but had the decency not to mention my father.

"Someone killed that priest," I muttered. I could see the gaping tunnel of crusted blood at the back of his head, so big in memory that I could have reached inside it, though in life it must have been no wider than a pencil.

"Someone," Rodger said. "But I'm still going on. I'll bet that's only a goatherd over there."

"No—" I started to say. This wasn't a game, not anymore.

He stared me down in the darkness, then I saw the glimmer of his teeth as he smiled. "You're such a girl, Peter."

After that, I *had* to follow him.

We picked our away along the path, still moving toward the glimmer of the distant cigarette. We had to cross a hundred meters of exposed meadow, clearly visible from the monastery walls. Silhouetting ourselves in the rising moonlight to the smoker in the bushes ahead at the same. The bet Rodger made staked our lives, but I wanted to believe what he believed, that something in New Albion was still normal.

Never in my life had I been afraid of my own home.

The smoking man was no less of a puzzle when we got close to him. For a moment I thought I was seeing one of the old statues, left behind by the Mayans before they had retreated to their jungle kingdoms far inland. He was short and wide, with an enormous nose and a high forehead. He wore nothing but a loincloth and a feathered headband. In the moonlight he looked as shiny and pale as the stones around him. Then his eyes gleamed as he took a drag on...what?

A small pipe, I decided.

Though he made no effort to block the path, we stopped in front of him. The land had risen again, hiding both us and the sacbe from view of the monastery, so we stood without fear of observation.

"*In la 'kech*," he said, in what had to be Mayan, waving the pipe at us. It was oblong, with the bowl carved out of the body rather than attached to it, and seemed to be made of jade. Whatever he was smoking was nothing like Papa's Gauloises. It was sweeter, more cloying, not at all unpleasant.

"Hey," I said. Beside me Rodger stirred, shifting his weight, but he had nothing to add.

There were stories, told by kids camping around midnight fires, of Mayan sorcerers who flew down from the mountains and spoke to goats and dogs before stealing babies. Everyone knew somebody whose cousin had lost a child to the native wizards. As I'd gotten older, I'd realized we told these stories out of guilt and fear.

The Mayan took another drag on his pipe. "You walk an old road." There was nothing wrong with his English.

"You're a long way from the mountains," I said, cautiously. Some few Mayans left their homes and crossed the coffee plantations to venture to New Albion from time to time, also to Teixeira and other cities of the Caribbean. Most were wanderers, poor or unhomed in search of work or shelter, but not all of them. Some were said to be princes, or priests, or great traders. Like all campfire stories, ours had held seeds of truth. For all the tales of terror, there were also rumors of young men given jade swords in exchange for a chance sharing of fruit.

"This is our land." He puffed on the pipe. "We cover it like the rain. You merely have use of it for a time."

"Peter," said Rodger, tugging at my arm again. He wanted to go on, to scout the monastery. Whatever he'd hoped for from this man wasn't to be found. But I was certain the Mayan had been waiting for us. I jerked my elbow free of Rodger's grasp and waited. Rodger huffed, but he stayed with me.

"*Tun*," said the Mayan. "That is Peter in my language. You are the stone." He laughed, and leaned down to tap his jade pipe against the first slabs of the sacbe. As he did a wind swirled up around us, circling as a dust devil will, though they do not blow at night.

"Peter." I remembered what I had been taught in Latin School. "The rock upon which Holy Mother Church was built."

"Your rock is foundering." He tamped some fresh crumbling herbs into his pipe, that the wind somehow failed to snatch away from his fingers even as it built stronger and stronger. "Your king is troubled."

"The alcaldé? He died some years ago."

Another puff of the pipe. The wind was like a wall around us now, green sparks flickering within its dusty flanks. I should have been afraid, but I was not.

"Your great king across the water plays at games," said the Mayan. "His games should not come to our land. In time rain always defeats stone, but sometimes only another stone is required." He handed me a feather which had not been there a moment before and smiled as the swirling wall of dust collapsed.

Rodger and I both coughed so hard that we staggered, blundering into each other as we wiped the grit from our eyes. When I could clear away the tears, the Mayan was gone like a ghost out of legend. I still had the feather in my hand, though.

"Look," said Rodger.

At our feet was the jade pipe, fallen inverted, a spray of crumbling herbs spread around it like a fan. A tiny jade idol, no larger than a saint's medal, lay next to the pipe. We both stared, each afraid to touch.

In the moonlight the idol was the very image of the Mayan. Had he ever been here? Or was there something in his pipe smoke?

"We can't leave those things lying around," I said.

Rodger knelt and gently touched the idol. It didn't spark or sizzle or snap at his fingers, so after a moment, he picked it up. "Pipe's yours."

I tried to scoop up the little fan of herbs, succeeded mostly in mixing them with dirt, but I refilled the tiny bowl. Then I plucked a few fresh leaves from a creosote bush growing nearby and sealed the herbs into the bowl before slipping the pipe into my pants pocket.

The feather I held on to.

"Death, then magic," said Rodger. "I will never forget this day."

"We'll see more death than magic before it's all over with," I replied.

Half an hour later we huddled in a bougainvillea, brushing against the hairy leaves. The sweet-smelling plants had grown up around a dead stand of scrub pines filling a gap in the ridgeline that sheltered the sacbe, almost due south of Our Lady of American Sorrows. We could get no closer to the monastery without walking up to the front gates.

By this time of the evening the air was cooling. I shivered, still clutching my feather, and stared across last few hundred meters at our goal. It remained brightly lit. This close, the details of structure were clearly visible. While the riverside, invisible to us, was sheer to Bullback Hill's cliff over the water, the side facing south had buttresses footed in the slope of the hill. These supported the wall, which was about ten meters high and quite smooth. The top of the wall was clear except for corner towers, where the Cistercians kept eremite's cells for contemplation. We were not high enough up to see over the walls to the buildings in the courtyard, but I knew from visits in better times that there were three floors of wooden galleries on the inside of the walls, with a stone chapel in the middle of the yard and various outbuildings.

Our Lady of American Sorrows resembled a fortress because it had been built as one, back when the British Americas Company had contested with the French, Spanish and Portuguese for control of the New World. The forests here had held mahogany and teak, there was more rain, and everyone had believed that the Mayans were wealthy with hidden gold.

In the end the Pope had settled affairs to his own satisfaction, the Mayans had withdrawn, and the fortress became a monastery where Cistercians prayed for forgiveness from the abused land and its absent people. But those monks had always kept their walls in good repair.

Nothing stirred there now, though the clatter of the diesel generator was quite loud from our little observation post.

"'Our king is troubled,'" I said under my breath. "What did he mean?"

"I—" Rodger started to scream, quickly cut off.

Feather still in my hand, I turned to look. Rodger's eyes rolled white and wild as a black-gloved hand covered his mouth. His assailant, all in black, held a knife at Rodger's throat. Another man in black with a machine pistol swung it back and forth, bobbing nervously, looking everywhere but at me.

"*À qui parliez-vous?*" whispered the man with the knife.

Though I knew very little French, Rodger had more, from his aviation magazine. He rolled his eyes at me, as if trying to make me speak by main force of will. I shook my head slowly. The man with the machine pistol nearly jabbed me in the stomach, but still didn't seem to see me.

How was this possible? I was right in front of them.

"*Dites-moi maintenant, petit porc, avant que je vous colle.*" The gloved hand slipped away from Rodger's mouth as his captor looked around, eyes darting nervously in the gleaming dark, settling everywhere but on me.

They were asking Rodger where I was. They had to be.

"Please, sir," my friend gasped.

Good, I thought, don't let them know you have some French. I was afraid to even breathe.

"I was just out looking for my dog," Rodger said.

"*Un chien?* This far from the city?" The man with the machine pistol spoke heavily accented English. He jerked the weapon toward Our Lady of American Sorrows. "*Nous le prendrons dedans.*" Both men laughed, then the pistol carrier added, "*Nous ne pouvons pas laisser un autre corps à trouver.*"

Even I knew what '*autre corps*' meant. Another body. So they wouldn't kill Rodger, not here and now. But they must have killed the priest in the river. And now someone knew about it besides us, or they wouldn't care about there being another body. Which maybe explained the shooting in the city this afternoon.

I shivered, torn between dread and disbelief, by some miracle standing unnoticed before these two dangerous men.

The knife vanished, and large, hard hands hustled Rodger over the edge, down the slope toward the monastery. The feather trembled in my grasp as I realized the two Frenchmen — Jesuits? soldiers? — had never seen me at all.

I was the stone.

After waiting a few minutes, I followed them down the slope. I picked my way carefully. Invisible or not, they could still catch me crashing through the bushes.

I almost caught up to Rodger and his captors just below the monastery. They had stopped at the bottom of a scree slope extending down from the roadbed, and seemed to be arguing. Rodger squatted between the two Frenchmen, who were pointing at each other and speaking in voices that I couldn't quite hear, even if I had understood them.

Rodger looked up to stare right at me. His face wrinkled into a sort of regretful smile, and he mouthed some word I could not catch. Then the Frenchman grabbed him, one to each armpit, and dragged my best friend up the slope to the roadbed and on to the monastery gates. Though I could still see no guards the postern opened as they approached. The three of them stepped through, Rodger making one last glance over his shoulder.

I picked my way up the slope much more carefully, wary of dislodging rocks. I was desperate to rescue my best friend but could not imagine how to get through the gate. Whatever invisibility the Mayan had given me did not allow me to fly, or withstand bullets. Or perhaps it would — but I had no way to test my powers except by trying.

The Mayan's words came back to me again. Was I the rock? Or was I the one who was foundering? Clutching the feather, I fingered the pipe in my pocket. There were still some herbs in the bowl, but they wouldn't help me cross the walls of Our Lady of American Sorrows.

If I went back to New Albion, I could ask Papa for help. But somehow his revolver was more frightening to me than a monastery full of armed Frenchmen.

The Pope's man, whoever had come on that jet. Cardinal, Bishop, Chancery Secretary. Some high official of the Church was present in New Albion. I didn't think he'd be out here at the monastery, either. I would take my feather and go find him on his aeroplane and warn him. Not even the Pope's emissary would be guarded the way Rodger was right now.

Someone had snuck these false priests into Our Lady of American Sorrows. Surely the Pope could have sent soldiers to New Albion openly if he wanted to.

But even though the Frenchmen had snuck in, the Pope's man had flown in for all to see, without stealth or guile. Someone of his rank would be a man I could trust, with authority to set things right. Heading back to the city to speak to him was the best way I could help Rodger right now. No one else had the power to rescue my best friend.

I wasn't happy with leaving Rodger, but there were none better that I could find. And I *had* to trust someone.

Then the gates squealed open and a truck rumbled out. Up close, I could see it was a Bedford truck, one of the Port of Ostia vehicles used to bring cargo into New Albion from the ships that called.

Surely this was a sign that I had made the right decision.

The truck rolled by slowly, the driver grinding the gears downward, so I grabbed at the stake sides and scrambled over the tailgate into the open bed. There was no one back there, but I shared the cargo space with several long, narrow boxes under a canvas tarp. I glanced at the cab. Two priests — or rather, two men in priest's collars — sat up front. I'd have bet they had machine pistols with them. Neither looked back, or even glanced in the mirrors.

I lifted the corner of the tarp and looked. The boxes were crates, soft, splintered pine stenciled with letters and numbers. In the last gleam from the increasingly distant monastery walls, I could read '*Missile Anti-Aérien.*'

More French I didn't need a dictionary to understand. This was what the false priests were here for: an assassination that would rock Avignon and bring disgrace upon New Albion. Now I had something concrete to say to the Papal representative, news about the trail his Comète would blaze when next it vaulted into New Albion's sky. I would trade that threat for Rodger's life.

The driver killed his lights and rumbled off the road just before we reached the edge of town. My ride was heading for the stony beaches of the river. I vaulted off the back, feather still gripped tight in my hand, and scuttled to the other side of the road to take cover in a line of tangled wild rose. The smell was clear and simple, slowing the beating of my heart, as I watched the truck lurch to the edge of the riverbed proper.

It stopped there, the driver shutting off the engine. I watched for a little while, but nothing more happened. Not even so much as a cigarette being lit. Who were they meeting? People from the shanty town? Traitors among the Civil Guard?

Could it be Papa?

It wasn't possible. Not my father. He worried about coffee prices and economic imperialism, not coups against the Church. Or by the Church, against the very government for which he worked.

Shivering now in the midnight air, I imagined an interrogation. Men in red robes from the Holy Office, gun-toting French priests and fat Civil Guardsmen with egg on their tunics would surround me.

"Would you call your father a *loyal* man, Peter?"

"Did he fulfill his duties to the city government?"

"What complaints did he voice about the affairs of New Albion? Londres? Avignon?"

"What about you, Peter? Have you been sneaking around in the—"

My head snapped up so hard my neck cracked. I was falling asleep on my feet, right here in the bushes. I couldn't stay still any longer. All I needed to was to drop the feather. Or worse, lose it. Mother Mary and the saints only knew how long the Mayan's spell would last. Rodger's life depended on me. If he still lived.

With a heavy sigh, I crossed myself, then trotted toward town. A man who came to New Albion in such a magnificent craft as that Comète would most likely sleep aboard, just like the Nord-américain tourists bunking in their cruise ships at Ostia. Our little hotels, the Hotel de la Réforme and the Ritz-Albion, were nothing compared to the luxury the Pope's man would be accustomed to. Even the Archbishop of Teixeira stayed at Our Lady of American Sorrows when he visited.

At this time of night our city's visitor must have been asleep. So I headed toward his jet aeroplane to see what I could do.

The landing field was no more than a long strip of dirt east of town alongside the road to Ostia. It had been bulldozed by the Brasilian army engineers during the Second Great War, back when I was a small child. The Brasilians had flown fat little gooneybird aeroplanes, as well as snarling fighters that I could still recall the sound of. Supposedly there was even an Ottoman squadron based here for a while, but no one I knew could remember ever seeing Turks or Arabs in the city.

Later the FEFA—Force Expeditionaire Français-Anglais—had liberated New Albion from the Imperialists. For a while a different set of fat little aeroplanes had flown in and out. The fighters had already moved on, following the front south and east toward the Brasilian heartland.

When the war was over, everyone had gone home, leaving New Albion with five captured Brasilian bulldozers not worth the trouble of hauling across the Atlantic as war booty. Now, fourteen years later, three of them still ran. They were used to maintain the road to Ostia and keep the landing field clear. The other two were parked for parts. Rodger and I had played on them for days on end when we were younger. Last winter, after the Boxing Day floods, I had even had the chance to drive one while working on the emergency road crew.

Now I approached the landing field, still clutching my feather. The two abandoned bulldozers bulked dark next to the equipment shed where the working bulldozers were stored. The equipment shed was an old coffee warehouse that had been dismantled and moved inland from Ostia during the Brasilian occupation. There was no light other than the naked bulb flickering over the office door — as Rodger had explained to me, no one ever flew to New Albion by night, so there had never been a need for landing lights.

Even while invisible I didn't know whether I would cast a noticeable shadow, so I was glad enough for the darkness. My sheltering shadow wouldn't last much longer, though. The three o'clock bells had rung in the Civil Palace as I passed through town along Water Avenue. Dawn would be coming in another hour or so.

The Comète was easy to find. The big silver jet gleamed in the waning moonlight. The door was open, a round-cornered black rectangle just behind the pilots' cabin. A coffee picker's three-legged ladder leaned against the hull just beneath the opening. There was a slight red glow from the cockpit windows, but otherwise the aeroplane was dark.

Too bad for me that a Civil Guardsman snored in a jitney parked under the wing. No, make that two, I thought. The second man was awake and smoking, leaning on a machine gun.

I was invisible, right?

Right.

Clutching my feather in sweaty fingers, I walked slowly, softly, across the dirt. I didn't want to kick a pebble or send up any little dust clouds in time with my footfalls. The man with the machine gun might see that, then see me. I kept a nervous eye on the wobbling glow as he took his cigarette from his lips, exhaled a cloud that gleamed silver in the moonlight, then resumed his smoking. I paused and waited to see if the coal would turn toward me, aiming like the barrel of a gun.

At least it could not be Papa. He was a bureaucrat, not a Civil Guardsman. He would be home with Mama, not shivering on a landing field this late at night. Though I wondered where he kept his gun.

Then I reached the ladder. I tested it with my hand. The wood shifted against the metal skin of the Comète. The coal of the Guardsman's cigarette shifted toward me, and I heard the muffled creak of the machine gun swiveling on its mount.

Nothing here, I thought. A stone. I am but a stone.

After a few moments, the cigarette began to bob about. The man in the jitney had lost interest. Very slowly I leaned on the ladder, bringing my weight to bear. It creaked, not loudly.

There was no reaction.

I eased my foot up onto the lowest rung. The ladder groaned, a noise like a door hinge! I jumped away from ladder, holding my breath against the effort.

The coal of the cigarette pointed right at the aeroplane again, and the Guardsman was muttering. How would I get into the aeroplane without him seeing me?

One man with a machine gun could not stand between me and my only hope of rescuing Rodger.

I made my way back across the field. I had to get the Civil Guard jitney away from the Comète long enough for me to board unnoticed. Once inside, it would be a different game, but I *had* to get in. Rodger's life was at stake, and the Frenchmen had taken missiles to the river.

What else could they shoot at but the Comète?

The office door of the equipment shed was unlocked, as it often was. Who would steal a bulldozer or a fuel tank? All the small tools were inside lockers of their own.

Inside was deep shadow. I could make out the bulk of the three bulldozers, a pickup truck, two fuel tanks on trailers, a forklift and lots of other heavy equipment—welders and drill presses and things for which I had no name. I went to the bulldozers. One was parked against the back wall.

Perfect.

Climbing into the seat, I reflected that this would not be so difficult. Electric starters had been installed after the war, in place of the old hand cranks. Mostly it was a matter of knowing what to do. Only seven months ago I had driven one of these, though Gomes the road boss hadn't ever let me use the blade.

I set the clutches for each track, pulling each long handle back and flipping the locking pawls. Then the transmission—left track in reverse, right track also in reverse. Pulled out the choke. Feather still gripped between my fingers, I put my fingers on the cool bakelite knob of the starter switch.

This was it.

I could still go home right now, but once I started the bulldozer, things would be different. They might never be the same for me.

Then I thought of Rodger sweating out his fear in some monk's cell. Or worse, under torture. The flame-tailed streak of a missile shooting toward the Comète. Papa's gun.

I wanted my home back. I wanted everything to be normal again.

I flipped the starter switch.

The electric motor groaned and chattered as it kicked the bulldozer's huge pistons toward life. There was a rattling cough, then the engine caught with a screeching roar. I tugged the accelerator handle, locked its pawl, and let the clutches loose before jumping out of the operator's seat.

The bulldozer clanked into life, back up to hit the wall of the equipment shed that faced the road. It seemed to pause for a moment as the building's beams groaned. Glancing up into a shower of dust, I ran for the office. The engine raced until the wall gave way with an explosive bang. I was out the office door at almost the same time as the runaway bulldozer backed its way across a narrow verge of struggling grass and into the road.

The smoking Guardsman was paying attention. I heard him shout, then the jitney started up. The gears ground and the coal of his cigarette jerked twice before the headlights came on and the vehicle shot out from under the Comète's wing to race across the landing field toward me.

I ran in a wide curve, staying out of the beam of the headlights. It turned out not to matter much—the equipment shed was collapsing with a great screeching of boards and rippling of the corrugated roof. No one would have noticed me anyway.

Panting from exertion, sweating even in the chilly air, I made it to the ladder at the Comète's door. No time to think now. I scrambled up, pushing through the door.

The feather in my hand caught on something and slipped free. I turned, stifling a scream, to see it flutter in the moonlight before it turned into a brilliant green bird that glowed like a little sun of its own. The bird rose above the landing field and flew toward town, and the mountains far to the west, a plumed Mayan missile.

Someone laid a hand on my arm. I turned to see an old man in a white cotton sleeping gown. He was very small, much shorter than I. His eyes were rheumed with sleep, bags of skin beneath them making him resemble a hound. He had a little black hat he'd apparently just pulled on over his short silver hair, and wore a jeweled gold pectoral cross.

A churchman then, and a wealthy one. Important.

"Can I help you my son?" He had an accent, something from Europe that I did not quite recognize.

"Father," I gasped, surprised to find my breath suddenly so short. "Pardon me. Lives are in danger. My friend Rodger's, and your own."

He glanced out the door at the ruckus around the bulldozer. "Step back here with me, son. We should speak."

I let him lead me along the red and gold carpet through a narrow door even as outside a machine gun stuttered once more.

The next cabin back within the Comète was a little sitting room of sorts. There were two seats on each side of the door we came through, facing back, and two more on each side of the next door, facing forward. They were oddly padded chairs, not quite like anything I'd ever seen, and both facing sets had a little table-topped cabinet between them. The tabletops were plastic, each with a small frame attached with several holes. This floor was also carpeted in more of the red and gold.

Somehow it was much shoddier and cheaper than I had imagined the inside of an aeroplane to be. Especially an aeroplane as grand as a Papal jet.

The churchman waved me to a seat. He bent down to open a cabinet. He removed two glass tumblers and a wine bottle, then set them in the holes of the little frame before taking the seat across from me.

"You have worked hard to come see me," he said, pouring out the wine.

I watched, fascinated. I was not permitted wine at home. "Yes...sir."

"What is your name, my son?"

"Peter." I was suddenly uncomfortable saying Papa's name, so I made up a last name. "Peter Fitzpatrick, of St. Cipriano's parish here in New Albion."

"Well, Peter Fitzpatrick, you may call me Father Kramer." Father Kramer, who was certainly a bishop or even a cardinal, handed me a glass.

"Drink. You must relax. Please excuse the poor service, we have no way to secure proper snifters aboard this infernal craft."

I took a tiny sip, as I had seen Papa do when he drank. The wine left a mellow, golden taste in my mouth.

"Thank you, Father Kramer."

"You are welcome, my son." He sipped at his glass. "So tell me of this danger."

"I— there are new priests here in town. False priests, Father." I would not repeat Mama's rumor that they were Jesuits. "They have taken the monastery. Our Lady of American Sorrows?"

Father Kramer nodded. "I am aware of the establishment. As for the new priests..." He shrugged and smiled. "The Cistercian Father Superior doubtless knows what he is about."

"The newcomers killed a priest there. And there are missiles, for your aeroplane."

"Ah." He set his glass down in the holder and leaned forward. "Dead priests. Missiles. Peter, Peter, my young friend. You have been reading too many of those dreadful Boy's Own adventures."

"I saw the body," I protested. After all I had been through to see him, how could he think I was lying? Father Kramer's doubt brought the sting of shame to my eyes. "The dead man was down at the river this afternoon. And the missiles, tonight, also at the river. These false priests have my friend Rodger imprisoned in Our Lady of American Sorrows."

"Ah." Father Kramer tapped his glass for a moment before raising his voice. "*Lugano, venite qui. Li ho bisogno di fare qualcosa.*"

Though I understood none of that, it sounded like the Latin of Mass, I thought as the door at the back of the little cabin opened. An enormous man in an undershirt and brown wool pants stepped out. He looked sleepy, except for his eyes which were bright like gems, and the pistol he carried. It would have been a huge gun for anyone but him, but it seemed lost in his large fist.

I felt as if I had reached for an egg and grabbed a snake.

"*Che cosa, signore?*" Lugano said. His voice rumbled like our river in flood.

"*Blocchi questo giù sotto.*" Father Kramer smiled at me, his lips pressed thin and pale. "*Rimarrà là fino a che non dica liberarlo.*"

Lugano stepped toward me, that gun staring me down like the eye of a dog. There was nothing I could do.

What did this mean?

"*Venite*," Lugano rumbled at me. "You come-a." The pistol cracked against the side of my head.

"*Non ci è necessità di danneggiarlo*," snapped Father Kramer.

Then Lugano tried to smile, which was almost more frightening. He dragged me back through the next door, through an unlit cabin with more seats set closer together, then past a few tiny doors until we must have been near the back of the aeroplane. There were several trapdoors set into the carpeting. Letting go my arm, Lugano opened the one closest to the back. He then poked me with the pistol. "*Sotto*. You down-a."

Down-a I went. He slammed the hatch shut, leaving me in the dark in a small metal-walled space that was empty of anything but me. Blood trickled down my right temple where Lugano had struck me with the pistol. I was more tired than I'd ever been in my life. All I could think of was the jet taking off from the landing field with me still in this little room. In my imagination, missiles rose from the riverbed on tails of flame to seek my life.

I shuddered with fear, fighting tears of pain, until somehow I fell asleep.

A clatter woke me up from a confused dream of the sacbe and the Mayan sorcerer and a flame-tailed missile that resembled a brilliant green bird. I blinked into a square of light above, partially blocked by a shadow that could only be Lugano.

Mama will be so ashamed of me. The thought seemed important and irrelevant all at once.

"*Affamato?*" he rumbled.

I decided the language must be Italian. No one spoke Latin but priests, and Lugano was no priest.

The big man tried again. "Ah, you ah eat, yes? *Mangia*."

"*Mangia*," I croaked. I was starving. More, I was thirsty. "Water, too. Please."

"*Si*." Though he was mostly shadow to my blinking eyes, I could see the gleam of his teeth. "Catch-ah."

A sack fell, hitting me on the head before bouncing to the floor.

"*Desiderate le sigarette?*"

Cigarette? I didn't smoke, but matches might help me better see where I was. "Yes, please,"

He tossed a cigarette pack and book of matches down at me, then leaned over with something. A glass bottle, I realized. I stood to take it from him, and discovered my little prison was no taller than I.

Once standing, I could see Lugano more clearly. He got to his feet and winked at me, then gently shoved the toe of his shoe into my forehead before slamming the hatch again.

It would have caught me on the head if he hadn't pushed me back down. I never imagined I'd be grateful to a man who held a gun to me.

Guns.

Papa.

Would he know where I was now? How would he find out? Father Kramer wouldn't think to tell Papa as I had given a false name. Rodger was in more trouble than I, and would be no help. No one else knew where I was except Lugano.

I had no doubts where Lugano's loyalty lay.

To take my mind from my troubles, I worked the cap from the glass bottle. I could not read the label in the dark. I would not waste matches on that. It hissed as it opened. I sipped to find mineral water. The sack contained two sausages and a small fruit with a nubbly rind, which turned out to be a lime when I tore the skin open. I ate everything but drank only half the mineral water.

Then I moved my hands around on the floor of my little compartment until I found the cigarettes and the matches. The pack rustled in my hand. It had been opened. I sniffed. The sharp, brownish-bitter smell of tobacco, but lighter and sweeter than Papa's Gauloises. I felt the rough heads of the matches. The matchbook seemed new.

I had already realized that no one was going to rescue me from here. I did not want to depend on Father Kramer's kindness. His Christian charity had been notably lacking when he'd had Lugano put me down here.

And why *had* he? Father Kramer knew about the missiles. He knew, and he didn't want me to know. Why would he plan to shoot down his own aeroplane?

Unless another aeroplane was coming. Surely not the Friday flight from Teixeira. That was due...I had to think. Tomorrow. The gooneybird would come tomorrow, with a few coffee factors or traveling priests or maybe even a confused tourist aboard. Who would care about them?

But another Papal aeroplane, maybe even another Comète. There would be death, and scandal. Armies would come to New Albion again, as they had during the Second Great War. We would be made part of Nouveau Orleans or British Miskitia. Papa would be sacked and Rodger and I would be made to fight. I couldn't—

I stopped myself. I could not know those things. I *could* know that Father Kramer knew of the missiles. I could know that he did not seem concerned for his own safety. Whatever plot was afoot was, in part, his doing.

And here I was, knowing where the missiles were, or at least where they had come from and where they had been last night. Papa or the Civil Guard could find the missiles, if only I told them. The ministerial junta at the Civil Palace could negotiate with Father Kramer, have him take his crime away to some other city. If only I told them.

Time to light the first match and look for a way out.

It struck easily and flared to life. The whiff of sulfur made my nose tingle even as I squinted against the brilliant glare. I was in a metal box, which I had already known from the feel of the things. The walls were seamed as if it had been welded from the other side. Any seam could be a secret door, but who would put a secret door in an aeroplane?

The match burned down to my fingers as I looked around. My prison was a little less than two meters high, just about as wide, and meter deep. I was going nowhere.

Shaking the last of the match out, I blew on my fingers to cool them where the flame had come too close. Soon enough nature would call. Especially if Lugano kept feeding me. That would be unpleasant in such a small place. After that, what else? Sit in the dark waiting for the missile?

I wished I'd kept the feather. Being invisible would not help me much in the dark, but while I was invisible, I had been special. Different. I had a sort of power.

Then I remembered the jade pipe in my pocket.

It still had the Mayan's herbs packed beneath the creosote leaves. I half stood so I could reach in my pants pocket and tug it out. The pipe was small and cool, its rounded edges comfortable in my hand. It was if the Mayan had carved the jade just for me.

I sat down again cross-legged like a tailor and tried to thread the needle of my thoughts.

What *had* happened on the sacbe? We met someone, for I had held the feather and still possessed the pipe. But the sorcerer had vanished like smoke, while Rodger and I were in more trouble than we'd ever imagined in our entire lives.

Our Lady of American Sorrows indeed. I was only learning what sorrows we Americans could have.

I didn't smoke. I especially didn't smoke herbs from some native's mountain temple. The thought was enough to make my skin itch. But where had he gone? What if the smoke was a kind of...a kind of, well, road.

Like the sacbe. An ancient, hidden road of the mind, instead of a goat track through the hills.

Carefully holding the pipe I tugged the creosote leaves free. I didn't want to spill the herbs. They were contaminated enough from the dust of the road. Whatever power they held might already be lost.

I set the pipe down on my thigh and struck a match. In the stinking flare, I noticed that the matchbook cover had a green rooster on it, with the name of some tavern. I took the green bird to be a good sign and picked the pipe up again. I had never smoked, but almost every adult in New Albion did. I had seen hundreds of pipes being lit.

Hold the match close. Take a gentle drag, pull the pipe away, exhale. Had the herbs caught? One more time with the match. Smoke came with that breath, almost choking me, but it was that sweet, cloying smoke that had wreathed the Mayan sorcerer's head back on the sacbe. It tasted...well, not good. Right, maybe.

Cautiously, I puffed again. My throat tickled, kept trying to cough, even as my nose started to run, but I inhaled the smoke. I didn't know what I was expecting — stone dragons, or an army of little men with jade swords. What I got was a lungful of smoke that almost made me cough all over again.

I bent over wheezing, trying not to joggle the pipe too much. I heard a flutter. As I turned to look I thought I saw a trace of green in the darkness of my little cell. Had the Mayan's bird flown by?

Another puff. Then another.

I smoked the pipe down to nothing. It did little but irritate my lungs. I looked at the little jade oblong, visible in the faint green light that filled my cell. It was nothing but a toy.

Why had I placed my faith in a nameless sorcerer? I'd never been invisible, just foolish. No one had met us on the sacbe except in a fevered dream.

Then I tried to close my eyes and rest.

There was another place on the other side of my eyes. I was still in my little metal cell aboard the Comète, but the walls around me were no more than a green fog. It was little different from my idea about the sacbe of the spirit. Everywhere I looked the world stretched before me like an open road.

The pipe had been no toy. I should be frightened, but that was not within me at that moment.

Above me and a little bit forward, I could see a soft green glow that I knew was the heart of Lugano. A hard glint hovered nearby. His pistol. Forward of that, in the next cabin that I could see three more hearts: Father Kramer and two men that seemed familiar.

The false priests from the truck with the missiles.

Somehow, they were together, Father Kramer and these men who sought to shoot down his aeroplane. Who was betraying whom?

They were all crazed, I decided, mad for power or God or the beauty of their weapons. Turning away from them, I looked further along the spirit road with my new eyes.

Southwest, away from the river and into New Albion, it was as if I watched fireflies in the spring. A whole city full of soft hearts and hard weapons, from the shanties by the river all the way up to the big houses on the tops of the hills well above our family's home. With that thought, I could see Mama in our house on Rondo Street. Then I spotted Father Lavigne, and Rodger's parents and his little sister, and down in his office by the river, Papa with his pistol at his side.

North of the river were tiny glows, the field mice and foxes of the scrubland, mixed with the larger, slower hearts of the goats and cattle that ranged there.

I looked west toward Our Lady of American Sorrows. The monastery was like a box of fireflies glowering with weapons. Rodger's heart still beat, a soft green lost in its depths.

And where were the missiles? If I could see the things I knew, surely I could see them. I looked back toward the river, scanning from the monastery toward town. It took me a little while but I found them, four lances of fire pulsing in the heart of shantytown.

Those two false priests in their truck down at the river had been waiting for the men who slept out on the beach. The men whose dosses and fires Rodger and I had passed by when we'd gone to search for this very aeroplane.

Seeing the missiles had drawn my eye back to the aeroplane again. Right before me, blooming with a fiery glare of hate, was something I did not understand. There were six hard-edged glints that somehow also shared the soft glow of the living hearts around me. Even as I watched their glow seemed to pulse higher, as if responding to my view.

They were inside the aeroplane with me, in a forward hold. With a sudden certainty I knew these were what had brought the Mayan sorcerer down from his jungle kingdom. These were the rocks on which my great king—the Pope—would founder.

I realized that they could be only one thing. Without considering what I did, I moved toward them, passing through the wall of my cell as if it were a fog. I stood among six long cylinders of some finely polished metal, carefully racked in the Comète's hold. There was a warning stenciled on the side of each.

Danger: matériau nucléaire. Ne manipulez pas.

Though I had very little French, it was as if a voice spoke within my head. *Danger. Nuclear material. Do not handle.*

These were atom bombs.

Some things are too dangerous even to put in textbooks. So ours, which came from Londres or Boston or Nieu Amsterdam, always years out of date, merely talked about the Pope leading the free world to a victorious peace in the Second Great War. But the headmaster at the Latin School, Dr. Souza, thought some things were too dangerous *not* to be taught.

This was not old history. Though I barely remembered it, the teachers at the Latin School had lived through the war. We were taught in fourth form, not out of textbooks, but simply from their mouths and old books of clippings and letters, wire recordings off the radio.

The Second Great War had ended abruptly after the French Armée de l'Aire had struck Sevastapol and Beirut with atom bombs. The shocked Imperialists in St. Petersburg and Constantinople sued for peace. With the collapse of the European Front, their Brasilian and Japanese allies were quickly forced to follow. The newly-elected Pope Louis-Charles III had gone on wireless and sworn on the blood of Christ never to use the terrible weapons again so long as peace reigned.

As Mr. Fentress had said in fourth form civics, if you thought about the exact meaning of the Pope's words, that pledge of peace was no pledge at all.

Now Father Kramer, surely acting on orders from the Pope, had brought those weapons to the Americas where they had never been before. Had brought them to New Albion, where they had never been wanted. Had brought his own stew of plots and counterplots to threaten us all.

No wonder the little man with the jade and feathers had come down from his jungle home. We were all lucky he had not arrived at the head of an army with demons on the wing. As a Catholic, I did not believe in demons. As an American, I believed in the natives and their powers.

"Sometimes only another stone is required," he had said.

I walked to the skin of the Comète and stepped through. Rodger and I had failed on our own, and I had lost him to the false priests. Father Kramer had betrayed me to a cell. I had only one place left to go for help.

Papa.

Moving through the green-lit town among the glowing hearts and shimmering guns, I imagined that if the people around me saw me at all I was no more than a bird to them. Perhaps it had been the sorcerer himself who had reclaimed his feather at the aeroplane's door last night. I found myself hoping he had watched over me since our meeting.

I flew along Water Avenue and lifted myself over the shantytown. The fiery lances of the missiles drew my eye again, scattered in four different places among the hovels of the poor. On foot, I was not sure I could find them again, unless some of the sorcerer's power were still with me.

It was enough to know that they were there.

Up the hill, I saw that Mama was making her way through the streets toward St. Cipriano's. She did not ordinarily go to Mass on Thursday morning, but with me missing and Papa working amid the crisis, she must have needed prayer. Or perhaps confession. If I'd still had hands in my bird form I would have crossed myself for her.

Then I was at Papa's office close to the Civil Palace. The Ministry of Commercial Affairs was one of the tallest buildings in town, four stories with cornices and limestone gargoyles over the high, narrow windows. Circling around it, I could see the hearts and weapons within. I saw that there were cellars, which I had never known, and more hearts beat deep beneath the ground. These were darkened or inflamed, hearts in pain, surrounded by more weapons.

Many more weapons.

Papa worked atop a prison.

I wondered at this. New Albion had one small jail, in the Civil Palace proper, where miscreants or drunks were kept. Serious criminals— murderers, rapists, incorrigible thieves—were sent to Teixeira to stand before the Archbishop's court. So we'd been told in Latin School.

But people disappeared some times. I knew this. Rodger's cousin's father had vanished while out hunting. Everyone said a jaguar had gotten him, but no body had been found. A man who lived further down Rondo Street had never come home from his job at the Coffee Exchange one day the summer I was fourteen. They said he'd been mugged and thrown in the river.

Oh, Papa. You lecture me on freedom, but you work atop a secret prison.

Still, who else did I have?

Even if he had turned into another man with a gun. I had come to fear what guns did to the men who held them just as much as I feared what they did to the men they were pointed at. There was no gun bigger than the atom bombs the Pope had sent to New Albion.

That thought decided me.

I circled the building twice more before I dove for Papa's window. The glass rippled against me as I passed through it, then I was in his office. He glanced up from his desk, looked at me without seeing me, rubbed his eyes and went back to studying some papers spread before him.

I found a perch on the back of a chair by the window. How would I speak to him? Would he believe it was me? I wasn't sure I was ready to give up the spirit road yet, even if I knew how. I did not think I could ever find my way back to this place, and I intended to go for Rodger once I had set Papa on the problem of the atom bombs.

The door opened and another man walked in. I recognized him as someone I'd seen in the halls here, but we'd never been introduced.

"*Fizeram-no*," said the newcomer. He was speaking Portuguese! The language of our Brasilian oppressors in the Second Great War. "*Os papéis em Teixeira e em Nouveau Orleans estão carregando a história, que significa que Londres e Avignon sabem tudo sobre ela.*"

Even stranger, I understood him, though I had no Portuguese. *They have done it*, he had said. *Everyone knew, even in Londres and Avignon.*

Done what?

"*Tolos,*" said Papa. *Fools.*

I had no idea my father spoke Portuguese. That chilled my heart.

"Idiots," he went on. "*Poderiam ter mantido esse segredo por anos. Uma explosão no Matto Grosso nunca observado. Mas preferem cantar como galos de um alto do celeiro.*"

No one would have noticed an explosion in the Matto Grosso for years, if they hadn't crowed about it like roosters in the barn.

Papa and the other had to be speaking of a Brasilian atom bomb. So the Pope hadn't been the first to bring those weapons to the Americas. No wonder the Mayan had come to New Albion. He needed to stop their spread.

"Now the bombs are here," I said aloud.

"Now the bombs are here," Papa said, echoing my words without seeming to hear me.

"What?" asked the other man.

Papa stared at him. "I didn't speak."

"You said something about bombs here."

"Atom bombs in New Albion," I said.

"Atom bombs in New Albion," Papa said. He clapped his hands over his mouth for a moment.

The other man frowned. "Are you well, Hubert?"

"I...I..." Papa never stammered, but he did so now. "I may have taken ill." He wiped his brow with a kerchief. "The pressure of the past few days."

"*Tenha um cuidado. Estes não são dias seguros.*" *Have a care. These are dangerous days.* He walked out, leaving Papa to stare at the wall.

I watched, wondering. Papa had never spoken Portuguese to me. He must have known something of the language, his mother was Brasilian, but Papa was born and raised here in New Albion. I never knew my grandmother. She'd died during the war.

During the Brasilian occupation, I realized, though Papa never spoke of it. What *had* happened to her?

Perhaps Papa was a spy.

Why would he be discussing explosions, in Portuguese, here and now? Because if he discussed them in English, too many people who might overhear would understand.

Neither Papa nor the other man had been surprised when Papa had repeated what I'd said about atom bombs. Surprised *that* he'd said it, yes. But not surprised at what he'd said.

Papa was a spy. Or a traitor. I glowered at him. The pistol had changed my father into someone I did not want to know. He had betrayed me as thoroughly as Father Kramer. My own father.

No one was what I thought them to be.

"Peter?" Papa whispered after a few minutes.

Without answering, I left the office. There was nothing I could do here. The world would have to save itself from an atom war, and my father with it. Rodger needed my help before the power of the spirit road left me.

My personal sacbe took me high into the sky and west, toward Our Lady of American Sorrows.

Approaching from the spirit road, the monastery continued to resemble a box of fireflies. I could see the lines of the buildings of the courtyard sketched against the outer walls. The beams of the structures were limned bright in my vision. Rodger was in a monk's cell in one of the towers. There was no one close to him, though the base of the tower was guarded. Trucks in the courtyard held more fire-lance missiles along with other weapons that glowed. Grenadoes, perhaps, or mines.

I did not want to know.

Instead I flew into the tower that held Rodger until I found myself outside his cell. I landed in the hall.

He lay on a cot, half sleeping. His heart flickered as if he were weakened or dying. There were no bars between us, just a wooden door someone had bolted from the outside. I had to go to him. I reached for the bolt to draw back, and in that single material act found myself off of the spirit road.

I was inside Our Lady of American Sorrows in the flesh.

For a moment I was angry at myself for letting the spell loose. How had that happened?

Because I was thinking of myself as being in the building, not on the spirit road, when I had reached for the bolt. It made me want to swear, that I had so easily given up the power lent to me by the Mayan.

Then I was amazed that I was there at all. This was a miracle of both God and sorcery, that I could come here to help Rodger in his extreme need.

And finally I was glad not to still be confined inside Father Kramer's Comète.

Enough. I was here with all my clothes and wits alike. I checked my pockets. The jade pipe was gone, as were the cigarettes, which of course I had not been holding when I'd smoked the pipe. I still had the matchbook with the green rooster on the cover.

I tugged open the bolt and stepped in to see Rodger.

He was pale, hot and sweaty. Both of his eyes were blackened. His cheek had been split, by a beating I supposed, and badly taped back together.

No wonder he was unguarded. Rodger would no more walk out of here on his own than he would fly without an aeroplane.

That was my department, apparently.

"Rodger," I whispered. "It's me. Peter."

"Ah..." he said. "I never..." He shuddered.

I felt cold, too, a freezing tang of fear like a dagger in my chest. I'd never seen a dead man before we'd found the priest in the river yesterday, and I'd certainly never watched someone die. But Rodger looked close. Too close.

"Don't worry. I'll get you to the Misericorde St. Cosmas in town. They'll fix you right up."

"Peter." Rodger's voice was a strained whisper. "The Pope, Louis-Charles...he's..."

"I know," I said, thinking of the atom bombs back at the landing field.

"They will kill him, I think." Rodger gasped. "So many questions."

Kill who? The Pope? Father Kramer? "Why the missiles," I wondered aloud.

"Cover their tracks." Rodger's breath heaved as his chest shuddered.

"Enough," I said. "Ups-a-boy." I gathered him up off the cot, his arm across my shoulder. Rodger couldn't quite stand, and his right foot seemed to be broken, but he held his weight on the left.

This was my fault. Everything that had happened to Rodger. I should have followed him into Our Lady of American Sorrows the night before. I shouldn't have left him here alone.

As we stepped out of his cell, I shot the bolt again. We shuffled to the stairs, he and I, and started down them. There was no one on the landing. When we made the next level down, the door at the base banged loudly and voices speaking French floated up the stairs.

"*...trois bataillons des parachutistes dans Teixeira,*" someone said. I could almost understand that.

They clattered up the stairs, a deeper voice complaining, "*Brésiliens damnés par Dieu. Teixeira est une ville ouverte. Aucunes forces là, par traité!*"

The first voice laughed. "*Aucuns militaires dans New Albion par traité, l'un ou l'autre.*"

The rest of them laughed at that too, five or six voices at least. They couldn't be more than a flight below us. I shoved at the nearest door, which popped open to the walkway atop the monastery wall. Rodger groaned as I dragged him out then pushed the door shut. We leaned against the wall, trying not to be seen from the courtyard below.

A few seconds later the squad inside the tower must have reached Rodger's cell. I heard someone bellow incoherent rage, then, "*Jésus Le Christ! Cette ville est-elle pleine des garçons d'oiseau? Ils toute la mouche foutue partie!*"

Some fragment of the Mayan's spirit road stayed with me, because I could swear I understood that. Bird boys, he called us.

Boys. Not boy. Which meant Father Kramer had told them of my escape. Of course, he'd had the false priests aboard the Comète this morning.

I smiled at Rodger. "We're going to fly out of here." I had no idea what to do next.

"Don't let them kill the Pope," he muttered, and sagged into my shoulder.

Craning my neck to look down into the courtyard, I saw two more of the Bedford trucks, loaded with weapons crates. A few real Cistercians scurried about down there, while a number of the false priests worked on weapons or exercised in a circle.

Though taking a truck would have been nice there was no way to get to it without being seen by the eyes of dozens.

I heard more shouting from inside the tower, then the door slammed open in front of me. Two of the Frenchmen raced out, rifles ready, right past Rodger and me. They looked over the wall at the river, then down at the courtyard.

We were trapped. Horrified, I prayed for some shred of the invisibility I had enjoyed the night before.

The two in front of us turned to face the courtyard, shouting, "*Avez-vous vu ce garçon? Le petit bâtard glissé librement!*"

A man cleaning a rifle pointed right at Rodger and me. He began to grin.

The two false priests turned. We weren't four meters apart. The one who had been shouting turned red, opening his mouth for some new round of insults even as the other raised his machine pistol at us.

We had seconds to live. Still holding Rodger's shoulder, I swept us both over the edge of the wall and into the air, forty meters or more above the river. I prayed for deep water and good lungful of air.

The last thing I heard was the surprised laughter of the Frenchmen.

When I'd flown out from town along the spirit road, that mystical sacbe the sorcerer's pipe had opened for me, I had been like a hawk or even an angel. I had soared above the earth with no care for the consequences of gravity.

It must have gone to my head, because for one tiny moment as we jumped, I somehow expected to soar again. Instead, Rodger and I tumbled out away from the wall and the cliff below, falling over the river as the dead priest must have a day or two before us.

We couldn't have been falling for more than a few seconds but I could have written books during my time up there in the air. There was a peaceful aspect to that moment of inevitability. Rodger and I were free of false priests and atomic bombs and my traitorous Papa, flying like birds. There were no more choices. We were committed, fleeing for our lives from bullets and bad intentions alike.

I had a brief hope that Rodger might have been free from pain too as he floated like a doll, loose in the air, when the flat hand of the river slapped us both into a deep, cold darkness.

My ears rang as hard as they ever had when I fell off a bicycle. All the air left my lungs in a rush. Even as my mouth opened to gasp, I stopped myself. I was deep down in the pool at the river's bend below Bullback Hill, the water almost black except for the pale curtains of bubbles. I wanted to swim, to find the surface, knowing I had seconds to live.

But where to go?

Even underwater I could hear. There were dull thuds, small sounds like raindrops in mud. More bubbles flashed around me, darting in lines.

Bullets. From above.

At least I'd found up. Which way was downstream?

I struck out for what I hoped was the base of the cliff, trying to get so close to the wall they couldn't see me from above. I needed to breathe with a dire desperation that made my body shake. Instead I swam. Still the water thudded with more lines of bubbles, but somehow none of the bullets found me.

Then I hit a rock head on and bounced upward only to bump something else which danced at my touch.

Rodger.

My face broke the surface just where his neck met his shoulder. Rodger floated on his back above me, dancing in time to the bullets striking his chest.

I finally cried then, not caring whether they could hear my sobs at the top of the wall, as I cowered beneath my friend and the bullets rained down on us from above.

After a while the lead stopped falling and the water carried us away.

"We're free, buddy," I whispered to Rodger a few hours later. I'd dragged him to shore about a kilometer upstream from New Albion, getting us both settled in a brake of juniper and low bushes.

Rodger had nothing to say, of course, but I had no one else to talk to.

Everything had failed. I could not stop whatever plot Father Kramer was up to with the atom bombs. Papa was a traitor and a Brasilian spy. If I'd understood what the Frenchmen were saying, and what Papa's friend had said earlier, the world was about to go to war again. Atom bombs in the Matto Grosso and Brasilian paratroopers in Teixeira.

The whole world was crazy and I couldn't even save my best friend. No wonder the natives hated us. The Mayans and all the rest had always known us Europeans were worthless. Rather than fighting, they simply had the patience to wait us out.

I didn't have that much patience. And I knew where some of the missiles were. Right in the heart of the shantytown.

"Rodger," I said, whispering to the ants already crawling in his ear. "I'm going to town. I'm sorry, but I have to shoot down that jet. I know you'll understand."

He didn't answer but I figured he understood.

My one advantage was that no one knew it was me who had been in and out of Father Kramer's aeroplane, then escaped from Our Lady of American Sorrows in a hail of bullets. The Frenchmen must have thought me dead, and Father Kramer only knew me as Peter. There were fifty boys named Peter in New Albion. Surely the plotters had larger concerns than their search for me.

So I walked down the road that became Water Avenue as if I had everyday business. I walked with the ox carts and the motorcycles and the taxis and everyone else just as if it were a normal Thursday in New Albion.

No one stopped me. No one looked at me.

Soon enough I would reach the shantytown. Any of those kids tried to hassle me, I would show them what real anger was.

It was enough to make me wish *I* had a gun, just like Papa.

Feral cats slunk along muddy rivulets between the ragged huts. Even in hot summer, these people managed damp and sticky filth. Small children with silvered hair sucked on their hands, staring at me, while larger kids of several races whispered and followed me and sent runners onward. There were almost no adults around, which surprised me. Everyone knew the people in the shantytown were lazy. If they were willing to do honest work they could live like honest people.

I supposed that some of them must work as maids or janitors or whatever, but why did they have to live *here*?

The shantytown wasn't really that large. It occupied a long, shallow triangle with the point out by the Bishop's Head, the flat side bounded by eight or so blocks of Water Avenue. But within that small space it was complicated. Tiny alleys wound into one another, too kinked and narrow to even ride a bicycle along. Buildings seemed to spring up every way I turned, while the whispering kids followed me, giggling.

I didn't know where the missiles were, exactly, but I knew they were here. I knew they were spread out. I couldn't be far from one or more of them.

Stopping, I tried to think. The power of the spirit road was gone from me. I could no longer see the lances of fire. But I had seen the crates they had come in. The missiles had to be over two meters long. Not something you could just tuck under a dresser. Some of these shanties weren't even that big.

"Hey."

It was one of the whispering kids. He had on a ragged cotton shirt and an old pair of underwear. He was barefoot, with dark skin, waxy-colored hair and green eyes, and could have been any age up to fourteen perhaps. A small fourteen. None of his kind bothered to go to school, so no one kept track. The whispering kid had his hands open, spread wide and facing me.

"Leave me alone," I warned. I tried to growl like Lugano, but mostly I squeaked.

"Oh, we are." He snickered, sounding for a moment just like Rodger.

I hated him for that.

"You looking for those Frenchies?" the kid asked.

Ah. The false priests had not made friends here. I woke from my stumbling rage, a little. "Yeah."

The kid shrugged. "They spread money around."

I'll bet they did. "Don't got no money," I said.

The kid shrugged again. "Some folks took it. Some turned away." He looked defensive for a moment, as if ready to fight at his own words. "We're New Albion, too."

"And the Pope is our—" *Friend*, I started to say, but I of all people knew that wasn't true. No friend of New Albion would have sent us such terrible trouble.

"Pope's a long way from here," said the kid. "Frenchies, they ain't so nice to us. Money ain't everything."

I was starting to understand how he thought. It seemed weird to say, even to myself, but I wasn't so different from this kid. "They leave something here?" I asked cautiously.

The kid nodded. "What you going to do?"

"Stop their crap."

"How?"

A good question. Smart kid. I hadn't thought about that. Hadn't thought beyond finding one or more of the missiles. I couldn't even see the airfield from here. Whatever the plot—and I still didn't understand it, exactly, but surely Father Kramer didn't plan to die—someone shooting at the Comète from here had to wait until it took off.

Up on the rooftop of, say, my house, you could see the landing field just fine.

I took the plunge. Everyone I'd depended on in life had betrayed me, so I would trust this kid, my casual enemy, instead. "Rondo Street," I told the kid.

"We know who you are. Meet you at the mills in the alley in an hour."

Because he was who he was, I asked the question I had to ask. "What do you want for it?"

The kid stared at me for a little while then laughed. "We are not beggars. Whatever you can do. Maybe just don't forget about us later."

These kids were going to steal missiles from the false priests for love of the city?

"I'll make it right," I said, flushing with shame.

I ran all the way home. Still no one looked at me. There were Civil Guard jitneys cruising the streets, but there was no shooting today. People clustered around newspapers or wireless sets, talking about war. No one but me seemed to know what was in the hold of the jet aeroplane down at the landing field.

As I ran I saw flashes of green in the corner of my eye, as if the sorcerer's spirit road were following me. Or perhaps just a bright tropical bird on the wing.

I burst into the house to find Mama cooking stew.

"Peter Ignacio Fallworth," she shrieked, "where *have* you *been*!"

I cannoned into her, hugging. "Mama." My voice was almost a sob. "Don't...don't..." I stepped back.

She looked at me. "My God, you've been, what, beaten? Did the Civil Guard do this to you?"

Looking down at myself, I realized that my clothes were muddy, bloody and torn. Mostly Rodger's blood, but still... "Mama. Listen. This is life and death. Make as much stew as you can. People are coming. We need to feed them, treat them like guests. I am going to give them my books, my lesson books and the others. My whole library. Please, please, if we have money in the house, we need to give them that, too."

"Have you lost your—" she began, but I interrupted her.

"Please," I said. "You must listen to me, Mama. I cannot explain now, but Papa is in trouble. New Albion is in trouble. The world is in trouble. I might be able to stop some of it. If I do nothing, it will all happen anyway." I took her shoulders. "Rodger is dead, Mama. I almost died. There are plots all over the city."

She screamed then, bringing her towel to her face. She quickly calmed herself and dropped her hands to her sides. "I would believe that you are mad," Mama said, "but I've heard that they found Brother Lazare in the river yesterday. And your father...I do not know how you knew of his troubles, but your father has been arrested."

Traitor. Did he deserve it? Had he been a jailor, or a prisoner all along? Or did this mean Papa was innocent? "Listen to what is happening in town, Mama. If you want New Albion back, do as I ask."

I ran into my room, leaving her to think. That is always best with Mama. She does not like to be pushed.

There I changed my clothes then grabbed all my books, even my treasured science fictions, and hauled them out to the dining table. I stacked them there and went back to my closet. I owned four pairs of shoes. I could give two away.

Papa's lectures on colonialism were finally making sense to me. We had made a colony of part of our town. If I was going to free the world from the Pope's atom bombs and Father Kramer's madness, I might as well start by freeing the poor of New Albion.

Rodger. I stopped, my breath shuddering. He would have been laughing alongside me right now. Clothes, then, and my Easter money, and my second-best ruler and protractor.

Back in the kitchen Mama had three stew pots going. "You are a man now, Peter, and I will trust you," she said without turning around. "See that my trust is not misplaced."

About an hour later a rubber-tired cart pulled by two mules trundled up the alley with a bulky tarp in back. The same silver-haired kid was driving. Three more kids from the shantytown rode with him on the board.

"Heavy," he said with a grin. "The mules, they are slow."

"Can we get the cargo up on the roof?" I asked.

The kid shrugged.

When the cart stopped, he carefully set the brake, then tugged the tarp free. There was a heap of trash in the bed. I opened my mouth to protest just as the trash cascaded off. Half a dozen more kids stood and stretched. They were all smaller than me, but as I looked at their faces, I realized they were my age or older.

Mayans? No, they were pale. Europeans, just as my family was. Just not enough food, like a dog raised half starving.

I was glad I could smell Mama's stew even from here.

The kids tugged ladders from their wagon, swarmed the wall of our house, and quickly brought the missiles out one by one.

This was the first time I had seen the weapons up close. Each had legs folded beneath it and sat in a sort of sleeve. They looked simple to operate. I hoped they were.

"Up, up, up," shouted the silver-haired kid. Within minutes all four missiles were out of sight.

"Tie your mules by the mills," I said. "We have a meal for you inside."

The silver-haired kid looked at me funny. "We don't eat up here."

"You do now."

They unset the brakes, moved the cart up the loading dock of one of the old mills, and set the mules by the horse trough. One of the kids filled the trough with water from the hand pump while I led the others inside.

Mama had every bowl in the house set out, the stew pots bubbling on her stove. "Welcome," she said with a fixed smile.

I was embarrassed, for everyone. What had I been thinking?

"Ma'am," said the silver-haired kid. He looked at me.

I nodded. I knew my smile was as tight as Mama's.

He took a bowl and dished out a few spoonfuls of stew.

"Fill it," said Mama. "There's plenty." Her smile was more natural now, perhaps at our guest's shyness.

"Thank you, ma'am." He paused. "Uh, I'm Reg."

"And I'm Mrs. Fallworth," said Mama. "Your friends are welcome to eat, too."

The kids from the shantytown fell to the stew like they had been starving. Which they had, I supposed. While they ate, I showed them my books, my clothes, everything I wanted to give them. "These are from Rodger," I said.

Reg looked at me over his emptying bowl. Around him the other kids, none of whom had said their names, slurped and spooned away at their stew. They stared at the two of us.

"Don't know no Rodger," Reg said.

"And you never will." The thought made me terribly sad.

"Can't take your stuff."

"Why not?"

"People will say we stole it."

I looked at the pile while spoons clinked. "But I'm *giving* it to you."

"Still say we stole it."

I was frustrated. I didn't know what to do. "I have to help you," I said. "You helped me."

"Don't forget us," said Reg.

"Peter," Mama said, her tone sharp.

Then Reg set down his bowl. "Roof time," he said.

They all set down their bowls, empty or not, and scrambled out of the house. I looked at Mama, who was picking up her rosary and shawl. She nodded at me, such small blessing as she could give.

I followed the little crowd out the door in time to see Reg fly backward off the roof and land hard in the alley. He sat back up and groaned.

Crud, I thought even as I scrambled up the ladder.

Lugano was up there with the missiles. This time he didn't have a pistol in his fist, but somehow he seemed bigger than ever. He also had a swollen nose and stitches on his lip.

"Pietro." His voice was thicker, too, as if he'd bitten his tongue.

"Lugano." I couldn't think what to say. "Welcome to my home."

"*Grazie.*"

He didn't seem moved to attack me. There was no way I could fight him anyway. He did seem willing to listen. I had to try. "What Father Kramer is doing...he's wrong, Lugano, very wrong."

"*È il mio padre. Devo seguirlo.*"

I almost understood that. "You don't have to do what he says, Lugano. Would God want what is being done here?"

"*Il Papa lo ha indotto ad essere. Il Papa* has made it be."

"This is beyond even the Pope, Lugano," I said softly. "Why would Father Kramer shoot down his own aeroplane? Who was going to be on it?"

Lugano stared at his feet, wearing the same pointy alligator shoes with which he had pushed me back into my little hole on the aeroplane. "Lugano."

Had he not known about the missiles?

He looked up at me again, his eyes smoldering. "Padre Kramer, he beat me, *lo ha battuto*, when you fled." Lugano touched the stitches on his lip. "He said I done it. *Regolili liberi.* Set you to free."

I tried to imagine Father Kramer setting on Lugano with a stick or the butt of a pistol. Lugano was three times the priest's size.

"I'm sorr—"

"He told me find you," Lugano interrupted. "But before, when we first have you, he told me *non ci è necessità di danneggiarlo.* To not-a hurt you." The huge man smiled. "So I find you. Still I no hurt you."

I glanced at the missiles. "Now what?"

"They think I am beast, big Lugano," Lugano said. "They talk before me. *Il Pape*, there is a...a...*cospirazione*...a plot. Not strong enough before the Turk, they say. Not stand up to the Russian. A man more powerful is-a needed. We make-a changes. *Il Pape* order Padre Kramer here with the big bombs to scare Brasil and the Turk. Padre Kramer say this is the time for change. He take the big bombs away from *Il Pape*, make himself the new *Pape*." Lugano stared down again. "It is wrong."

"That's what I said." The coup wasn't against New Albion, I realized. It was against Avignon, against the Pope himself, using the nuclear weapons as a lever of some sort. There were plots and more plots afoot. No wonder the Brasilians had moved against Teixeira—they must have gotten word about the atom bombs being here. Despite the cold fear in my heart, I kept my voice soft. "You don't have to do this. Any of it. This is wrong, wrong enough to kill the world."

"I will not. But you no hurt Padre Kramer. This Lugano cannot do."

I walked over to the missiles, glanced back to see Reg and the other kids at the edge of the roof. They watched Lugano nervously.

The Comète was visible, right where I expected to see it. One shot, maybe two. The false priests—Father Kramer's men—had more missiles at Our Lady of American Sorrows. They still had their plot, shooting down the departing aeroplane to cover Father Kramer's tracks. Everything would be blamed on us here in New Albion, or perhaps the Brasilians.

A perfect excuse for a war, I realized, and confusion for that coup against the Pope. Father Kramer would be hidden here at Our Lady of American Sorrows, with his terrible weapons ready to be used.

But I had missiles too. Father Kramer and the atom bombs were still on board. I only had to get around Lugano and I could destroy—

Then I realized what I was thinking. Just as the pistol at Papa's belt had done to him, these missiles were making me into someone I didn't wish to be. The Mayan had wanted me to solve this problem, but surely he had not wanted a battle.

The bells struck the hour across town, at St. Cipriano's and the other churches and down at the Civil Palace. It was three in the afternoon.

Bells.

"Reg," I said. "Lugano and I are going to the middle of town. There will be a disturbance. When the Civil Guard is busy with that, take as many people as you can find and mob the landing field. Stand close to the jet, don't let it leave. *Don't* fight them. You will just be shot. Can you do that?"

The silver-haired kid nodded at me, suspicious. "Yes. Can you?"

"I think so, but I'll need your cart. I must take a missile."

Lugano walked over to the weapons, leaned down and picked one up. The strain made the tendons of his neck stand out, but he managed it. "I carry one. Enough?"

"Enough," I said. "No cart, then. We need to go to St. Cipriano's now and see Father Lavigne."

Once we climbed down from the roof, Reg wrapped Lugano's missile in the tarp from the rubbish cart. It looked almost as if the big Italian were carrying a coffin. The shantytown boys took their cart and left while Lugano and I trotted to St. Cipriano's. Mama was nowhere to be seen.

"You want *what*?" Father Lavigne demanded, glancing nervously at Lugano.

"Ring the fire bell," I said. "Get people in the streets. The other churches will pick up the peal if you begin it."

"But there is no fire."

"There will be," I said darkly. "There is a plot against the Pope himself, and it has come to New Albion. We can stop it now, peacefully, before the next Great War breaks out. But you need to ring the fire bell to begin things."

Father Lavigne shook his head. "Peter —"

Then Mama stepped through the church doors and took the priest's hand. "Peter is touched by God this day, Father. Please. You have known us for many years. Hear me. Please. My husband is in prison, the city is in danger. My son, maybe he can save us."

"The Archbishop will have my head," said Father Lavigne, but now he was nodding.

"As soon as you can," I said.

"*Grazie*," Lugano added.

As we ran toward Water Avenue, I asked the big man, "Do you know how to shoot that thing?"

"*Si.*"

"Is it big enough to destroy a building or something?"

"No." He considered that as we jogged along, tongue sticking out of one corner of his mouth. "Make a big hole in a wall, maybe."

Perfect. I knew exactly what I would do. "I will show you the target, then."

We came out onto Water Avenue near the Ministry of Commercial Affairs. I tried to imagine the layout as I had seen it from the spirit road, the people in the cellars. The prison where Papa was. They had been below the entire width of the building. Where would 'a big hole in a wall' do them, and Papa, the most good? After a moment's thought I pointed out a series of tiny windows set at street level, admitting light for what I had always thought were storage rooms. They stretched to each side of the main entrance.

"Can you hit one of the windows mid-way between the entrance and the corner on the right side?" I hoped to God no one was in the cell we would be aiming at, especially not Papa, but I had to hit it somewhere. Then the prisoners could escape, carrying my father and their stories with them.

"*Si.*" Lugano grinned, set the missile down, and pulled the tarp off.

People immediately drew back from us, muttering, but then the fire bell began to ring at St. Cipriano's. Two Civil Guardsmen came out on the portico of the Ministry building and stared at us.

The legs snapped into place on the launcher's frame. Lugano grunted as he lifted the back end off the ground, essentially leveling the missile. He opened a little panel in the sleeve and toggled two buttons. "*Un momento.*"

"One moment is all you're going to get," I said, watching the Civil Guardsmen draw their pistols and start toward us. The bells at Santa Clara and All Angels' picked up the fire signal almost at the same time, though the carillon at the Civil Palace was still silent. I stepped around the missile and put myself between it and the approaching Guardsmen.

"Hey," said one of them. "Aren't you Hubert Fallworth's kid?"

The other looked thoughtful.

"Down now," said Lugano in an ordinary voice.

I dropped to the cobbles, slamming my knees and elbows painfully onto the ground as the world roared and flame washed across my back. A moment later the earth tossed me upward in perfect silence.

Something was wrong with my ears.

A shadow flashed over me, a big man practically in flight.

I sat up to see Lugano fighting both of the Guardsmen. The missile's launch frame lay toppled next to me. I put one hand on it to support me as I rose, but it burned me.

I held on despite the pain in my palm. I could barely stand as it was.

"Hey," I shouted, but I could hear nothing.

People were running around with their mouths moving as if they screamed. Smoke billowed from the Ministry of Commercial Affairs, much more than I would have expected from one big hole in a wall. Everything was quiet as midnight.

Something was definitely wrong with my ears.

"Hey!" I shouted again.

Lugano finished knocking heads together, came and picked me up to sit on his right shoulder. I could feel him shouting, feel the muscles move in his neck as he yelled. People stopped running, turned to face him and me.

"There is a coup," I said as loudly as I could, though I could hear nothing. These people wouldn't understand about the Pope, but they would understand about New Albion, since the shootings this week. "Some of you go into the basement of the Ministry right now. Some of you go the landing field and search the aeroplane right now. Everyone must know what is being done to us."

I could see the crowd twist and turn, like an animal searching for its tail. They were worried. They were afraid. I could only imagine the noise of their panic, though I could hear none of it.

Then they went. First a trickle, a few men picking their way into the smoke and dust of the shattered façade of the Ministry building as others began to stumble outward from the wreckage. Some more men began to head east, toward the landing field. More followed. The trickle became a flood, and then it seemed like half the city was on the move.

By the time the Civil Guard arrived in force to beat Lugano and me into submission, the real fight was over. I was happy to be arrested by New Albion's Guard because it kept me away from the false priests with their machine pistols.

I was more happy that I had not become another man with a gun.

A green bird came to me that night in my cell beneath the Civil Palace. There being no more prison for the politicals, they'd put me in with the drunks. I didn't know where Lugano was, but I hoped he was going to be all right.

Three men snored on bunks around me, though I still could not hear. A fourth sat and muttered at the wall, which made my deafness a blessing, though I prayed that my affliction was temporary. None of them noticed when the bird flew through the barred window, circled the cell twice, and came to rest beside me.

I smiled at it, having little to say. Everything was out of my hands now.

The bird looked at me, cocking its head as if to see if the view differed between one eye and the other. It glowed slightly. I thought I could see the ripple of its heart. Then the bird shook itself, leaving me with a tiny jade idol in my hands as it vanished in a cloud of sparkling green dust.

Save for the idol, it might have been a dream. I did not look to see if it more resembled Rodger or the sorcerer. Instead I kept it pressed between my hands, expecting no magic and finding none.

My memories were enough. I thought about Rodger and prayed to St. Cipriano for my friend's soul.

Later, Papa came for me. His white shirt was spattered with dust and blood and stained with smoke but he was smiling.

Nothing was said as the Civil Guard brought me from my cell, but I found I could dimly hear the clink of keys. On the long walk home, Papa began to talk about coffee mills and pressing the beans and what he hoped his redesigned mill would do for the economy of New Albion. His voice was tinny and high, but I was glad to hear it. Trucks rumbled past us through the streets, filled with straight-backed men heading for Ostia, but I did not need to look to see who they were.

Rodger would rest little more easily.

As we walked through town in dawn's first light, I even heard a distant roar. The Comète rose from the landing field, banked above the town, and flew away. No tongues of fire followed it, no missiles deadly and true. I knew with a certainty that the beating green hearts of nuclear fire had left with Father Kramer. If there was going to be another Great War, it wasn't going to start here in New Albion.

Papa nodded at the aeroplane. "Your large friend," he said, interrupting his own lecture on milling and grinding, "he has stayed behind, throwing himself on the mercy of the abbot of Our Lady of American Sorrows."

I smiled, knowing Lugano would safe.

At home there was nothing to do but put the jade idol away and listen to Papa rant about coffee and colonialism. He did not mention Brasil and I did not ask about his speaking Portuguese. I rather imagined I'd find myself before the ministerial junta before too long and did not want to know any more. Rodger would have his funeral soon, while I had unfinished business of a friendlier sort in shantytown. There were American sorrows enough for me to face.

It was enough for today that my father wore no gun, and that I wanted none for me, and that a green bird flew free and happy in the dusty summer skies of New Albion.

daddy's caliban

Mommy always told me and Cameron not to go looking for ways to reach the Old Tower. "There's ghosts and worse over there, Henry," she'd say. "You boys got to go wandering, fine, you're boys. But our people stay on this side of the river. Better yet, stick to the park."

The park was safe but dorky. When we were seven, that was okay.

This side of the river was home, Mabton and everything that was ordinary. When we were ten, that was okay.

Summer we both turned thirteen, well, there was nowhere else to go but across the water and up the hill. Mama must have known that—all us Puca boys got the wander in us, as Daddy says, but she just wagged her finger and warned us off, then packed sandwiches and said to stay out until dark.

Daddy worked in one of the mills north of town, where the river drops through a series of falls and they could put in big waterwheels a hundred years ago. It was all steam engines and belts now, but that was where the buildings still were. He was a shift supervisor at Caliban Products, which meant he hassled the other kids' moms and dads about being late or taking too long in the can.

Mommy don't work. Daddy said she couldn't work down at Caliban, against the rules, and he wouldn't let her work for the competition, so she stayed home and ground peanut butter to sell at the farmer's market on Sundays and knit scarves longer than Daddy's pickup truck for church sales. She spent her free time hollering at me for tracking mud in the house and such like.

Cameron wasn't exactly my brother, really. He was Mommy's sister's kid, her twin that run off before I can remember, but nobody would ever say who his father was, or even talk about him, so I figured maybe it was Daddy. Me and Cameron looked a lot like twins ourselves.

Cameron lived in a little room in our basement, and never sat down to dinner with us, though Mommy left food out for him. She always shushed me when I talked about him around other people. He wasn't allowed to go to school with me, either. Which always seemed weird, because wasn't like there were a lot of kids in Mabton to start with. It's town full of grown-ups. There were plenty of empty desks down at the school.

Somehow, though, when Daddy got me a bike down at the People's Collective, he always came home with two. Somehow when Mommy finished going through the shoe bin down at Ladies' Aid, there was always a pair for Cameron.

He was the kid who wasn't there. Mommy said I was the kid who was never anywhere else. Maybe that was why me and Cameron got along so well. We were like ink and paper.

River's hard to get across. Ain't no bridges to the other side. Every now and then somebody ran a piece in the *Argus-Intelligencer* complaining of the fallow fields that glisten with morning dew, or the woodlots just waiting to be put to the axe, and maybe we should have a ferry or something, but there's 'reasons.' The kind of reasons nobody told kids like me about, not even in school. They sort of oozed into me anyway, on account of those reasons were as deep in the bones of Mabton as the old trolley tracks under the street pavement.

Mostly, though, that river was out of mind. Except where the land flattened out downstream by the mills, there was a bluff right along the riverbank that sloped back down into town. Like maybe the river's course had been through the middle of town once and that bluff was an island. I guessed that's what kept it out of the Letters page of the paper—too much trouble for most people to bother with after a hard day's work. You had to climb the bluff to get a good look at the river and the fields beyond, and the hill above the fields, and the Old Tower high on the hill. Except for the Old Tower, gray stone with no roof poking above it, tilting slightly as if the tower had cause to fight the wind, the other bank of the river could have been the Garden Beneath like we hear in the stories at Saturday School.

Me and Cameron liked to sit inside the rhododendrons up on the bluff and spy on the deer that come down to drink in the river on the other side. Some of them were white as hutch rabbits, the bucks with racks wider than we were tall. Them pale deer wouldn't last a season on this side of the river what with rifles and hunting licenses. Over there...well, I believed it just might be the Garden Beneath, like Mother Arleigh always read to us about. Except in real life no one ever seemed to cross back into the Lands of Promise.

That didn't stop us. We sat in the bushes and whispered plots against the river.

"Maybe we could just swim."

"Current's too strong."

"How do you know?"

"Throw a stick in, dumb butt." Twinsies or not, Cameron had a harder mouth than me. Maybe that came of living next to the furnace. "Watch it go. That'd be you, screaming all the way down to the mill dams and the water falls."

Cameron was smarter than me, too. I wouldn't have thought of that thing with the stick. I worked at the idea a bit. "What if we start real far upstream?"

"Don't matter if you can't swim hard enough to cross the current."

"Ropes."

"What good's a rope unless you can tie it off on the other side? Where we ain't. Besides, where would we get ropes that long?"

He was right about that, too. The river was a hundred yards wide if it was an inch, counting the swampy bits at the foot of the bluff on our side, and the dark pools at the feet of the willows on the other.

"Rafts," I finally said. I was proud of that one. "We could build a raft."

Then the afternoon whistle blew down at the Boott Mills, always seven seconds ahead of the hour as Daddy liked to complain, followed by Caliban and the other mills. The busses began to grind people home in slow blocks as we ran back, me to Mommy cooking dinner in the kitchen and Cameron to his saucer of milk and plate of warmed-over scraps in the basement.

Mother Arleigh had a face like a peachpit, but she was sweet as ice cream most of the time. Her wimple never seemed to fit her right, and I always figured deep inside all that service to the Lady and prayer and everything was some ancient little kid who wanted to ride the swings right past the puking point just like the rest of us. Sad part was, that same lost kid part made her bitter-mean when she wasn't set to be kind. Like Mommy's blender, Mother Arleigh only had two settings.

That Saturday she was on the bad one.

"'Suffer the little children,' it says here," she screeched, banging the Scriptures so hard that her lectern wobbled. One of the felt angels slid off the teaching board behind her. "Well, I'm not going against the Lady's word." Her voice dropped to a hiss. "So which one of you little apes put soap in the tea kettles in the church kitchen?"

To a kid, the eight of us giggled.

I mean, who wouldn't?

The church bulletin from last Saturday had said this week's Saturday School lesson was the Seven Secondary Virtues. I had spent all week memorizing them, writing the list of Virtues out on the backs of gum wrappers and inside the folds of those little napkins from the ice cream truck. Soap in the tea kettles wasn't a virtue of any kind, but it was still pretty funny.

"Smart alecks," Mother Arleigh snarled. "Ruined six ounces of perfectly good Siamese green." She banged the lectern again. "*This* isn't what the Lady meant when she told us to keep clean tongues in our heads."

She didn't intend the joke, but we all fell out laughing just the same. Mother Arleigh's pinched face turned the color of my old wagon, and she commenced to whaling into us with the pointer she used for the felt board lessons. "I will teach you all to mind!"

The pointer got me hard on the elbow and I busted out into a shriek despite my desperate thirteen-year-old resolve to be cool. Mother Arleigh immediately dropped to her knees and gathered me in an awkward hug. "Henry, Henry, please forgive me my boy," she said, her voice a whisper burred by tears.

She wasn't angry no more.

"Hey," I said, trying to push her away, but Mother Arleigh grabbed on to me harder, until the other kids laughed at *that*.

Instead of blushing into her scratchy old wimple, I concentrated on the Seven Secondary Virtues—evenhandedness, punctuality, orderliness, patriotism, thrift, industry and cleanliness. Their first letters made a little word that helped me remember them in order. "I am epoptic," I whispered, as Mother Arleigh's dry old lips smothered me with kisses and she wept like I was her own baby lost.

Later, we had services. Daddy wasn't there, and of course Cameron never came, but Mommy smiled up at me in the men's gallery from her seat in the front row.

Sometimes, at services, and once in a while at home, I would catch her in the corner of my eye and see someone else. It was like Mommy was bigger than she was, something huge and substantial that had set a fingertip down into this world.

Then she'd laugh, or roll her eyes at some monkey-clowning of mine, and she was just Mommy again.

That day at church, she was big every time I looked away from her. It was like having an invisible mammoth in the room, huge and hairy and warm, with tusks longer than an automobile and breath like a dying swamp, but you never could quite see it, even when you had to step around it.

Maybe it was Mother Arleigh's homily. She had her vestments on now, white robes trimmed with gold, her silver athame and her golden sickle dangling from her belt. Her pinched little face glowed with the light of the Lady as she talked about the Lands of Promise and the fate of the Lady's people.

"When we left the Garden Beneath, we were wrong." Her voice was sweet and smooth, like honey on bone china at solstice feast. She paused, staring out over the women of the congregation on their crowded benches, all dressed in their Saturday best, then up at us in the men's gallery.

Though 'us' was just the few boys from Saturday School and a pair of truckers in from their long-haul sheep run looking for their Saturday prayers. Local men didn't like the services much. There weren't enough local boys for me to get away with skipping.

"Not many are left of us who can recall the Bright Days, let alone the Garden Beneath. There are few enough who have even heard the stories first hand. Our people did only one thing *right*." She banged her fist against the pulpit, which boomed like a drum.

"We asked the Lady for a promise. In Her wisdom, She heeded our prayers. Even though..." Another round of staring. "Even though we were *fools!*"

"Fools!" shouted some of the women below. Mommy just wore her little smile.

Mother Arleigh raised her hands in burgeoning ecstasy. "Who remembers the brilliant banners, the horses running like wind before a storm?"

"I do," called old Mrs. Grimsby, who most days couldn't remember to wear her underthings on the inside of her clothes.

"Who remembers the days of our power, when the swords of our men and the words of our women were the writ unto the uttermost corners of the sea?"

"Yes!" screamed one of the women. "I do! I have dreamed on it!"

I didn't know her, but I was fascinated when she jumped up out of her pew and began rolling in the aisle.

"We were there. We were all there. Na ba lo ka ti ko na! Hai ba la ba ko na!" She commenced to shrieking and crying.

"Miss Blackthorn has been touched by the spirit of the Lady," said Mother Arleigh, settling her hands back to the pulpit. Her voice was almost normal. I realized she didn't want to compete. I'd never considered services that way before, and it made me uncomfortable.

We all watched Miss Blackthorn writhe around shouting for a while. She slipped almost out of her clothes, which I thought was the most interesting part, then two of the other ladies finally led her away.

Mother Arleigh looked around. Her fingers drummed on her pulpit like a death march. Mommy still had her little smile though most of the women were downcast now. I kept seeing my mother's flickering hugeness in the corner of my eye. Was it the homily? Or was something wrong with me?

"We all know the promise. We all know what was given to us, to our ancestors, to *you*, Mrs. Grimsby."

"Praise the Lady!" shouted Mrs. Grimsby.

"Praise the Lady," echoed Mother Arleigh. "We were given what?"

"The Lands of Promise," all the women shouted, even Mommy. Some of the boys around me started giggling, but not me. This was the best kind of service, on those rare weeks when they really got going like this.

"When was it given to us?" Mother Arleigh called.

"When the end began!" they responded.

"When will we receive it?"

"When we have earned it!"

"And have we earned it yet?"

The women burst into such a lot of howling and cursing that it was fit to deafen me. 'Caterwauling,' Daddy called it, which was why he mostly went down to the Switchman's Rest and drank with the rail workers on Saturday morning. He didn't hold with mixing with his mill workers.

I watched Mommy, who sat still smiling as the rest of the women were on their feet, shaking loose their hair and tearing at their clothes, wailing death chants and curses. Mommy seemed bigger then, right before my eyes instead of in their corner, but at that moment Peggy the altar girl tugged the curtain into place and shooed us all out of the men's gallery while the women practiced their ancient mysteries to much screaming and howling hidden from us below.

Danny Elphinstone had tried to peek in the church windows once, when the services had gotten hot and heavy like today. He'd been struck blind and dumb and had to be sent away for three months to recover. When he came back he didn't remember none of his friends. Like a whole new kid, with blank spots.

Me, I scampered home to Cameron to plot against the river. When I got back, there was note on the nail on the back door, in Mommy's handwriting.

Henry — Baked potatoes in the bucket on the stove. Make the best of your day. Don't go near the Old Tower.

"Rowboats," Cameron said as he gnawed on a scrap of potato skin.

"Rowboats?" We'd been counting the fish jumping on the river, in between straining our eyes for the distant, snow-capped peaks that could sometimes be glimpsed rising above the hills on the west bank when the weather was just right and the air was heartache-clear.

"We could get across in a rowboat."

"That ain't no different than a raft," I complained.

"Sure it is." He grinned, his clever-ape grin that let me forgive him any annoyance, then held up two fingers. "First, we don't have to build it like we'd have to build a raft. Second, rowboats have oars. We could get across the current."

"And where are we going to get a rowboat?"

He just stared at me, still grinning. It was something obvious, something he knew and I should have known.

Then I shivered. The mills.

Some of the mills, Daddy's Caliban included, kept little boats for inspecting their discharge pipes and checking the surviving old waterwheels that sometimes still creaked like the walking dead.

"We can't do that," I said.

"Why not? We stole Timmy Grapevine's scooter last spring."

"Yeah, but we gave it back three days later. And Daddy doesn't work at Timmy Grapevine's *house*."

If we stole from the mills, any of them, not just Caliban, and got caught... I couldn't even imagine the shame. Or the beating Daddy would give me. And for something like that, Mommy wouldn't stir to stay his hand. She'd just smile and shake her head. I could foresee the consequences of failure with the same certainty that I could foresee the sun rising tomorrow.

"So you're soft now, Henry?" Cameron leaned close, until I could smell the sour milk and coal dust on his breath. The warmth of him made the little hairs on my arm tingle. "River's too much for you, got you scared."

"No." I pushed him away, hands to his chest. A spark popped between us, like winter static, a tiny glare of blue that surprised me though he didn't seem to notice. "I ain't scared. I'm sensible. Besides, we can't take a boat from the mills. We'd have to haul it two or three miles upstream to be sure of getting across before the current took us down to the mill dams and waterfalls."

Cameron's grin stretched so wide it threatened to split his face in two. "Bluff'll hide us from view, once we get away from the mills."

"We don't have the keys," I said. My ground was getting weaker, I knew. "Those fences are topped with razor wire."

"Your Daddy's got the keys to Caliban."

Our Daddy I thought. On days like this, Cameron was like me in a black mirror, every nasty thought I ever had seeming to fill his head.

"We'll be lucky if he kills us."

"Then we just won't get caught, will we?"

The other side of the river. I looked across the water. The fields gleamed in sunlight, the forests beckoned with their cool green halls. Above it all the Old Tower rose like a finger pointed toward Father Sun. In that moment, I could even see the crisp snowcaps of those distant mountains to the west. Something glinted from high up in the Old Tower.

That decided me.

"I know where Daddy keeps his work keys on the weekend," I said.

Cameron hugged me. "That's my Henry."

Did I love him or hate him, my almost-brother? I couldn't say as I gathered the pail and the napkin and picked my way down the slope, through the scrubby forest of little, twisted pines and silver-barked aspen toward the streets of Mabton and our small house.

Our family lived in a frame house on a brick foundation. The basement was low-ceilinged, dirt-floored except for the brick pad under the furnace and the little utility rooms where Cameron lived and where Daddy stored his tools. Everything else was a domain of sacks of half-rotted root vegetables, old crates and straw bales and an endless war between rats and cats.

Where the underside of the house was like a little nightmare with Cameron as the demon at its heart, upstairs was pin-neat and ruler-straight. Mommy didn't believe in dirt. With the time Daddy's job forced upon her she proselytized mightily for the forces of cleanly order. She was the Seven Secondary Virtues in the flesh.

It wasn't a big house—two bedrooms, a main room and the tiny kitchen, plus the indoor bathroom that had once been a porch and was now Mommy's pride. I knew other kids, like Peggy, lived in brick houses with two or even three bathrooms that had heat in them in the winter, but her father was a judge and things were different for people like that.

We were proud of who we were and what we had. Mommy filled the place with flowers and twisted sticks and odd charms that people like old Mrs. Grimsby made her, plus the curious little misfirings that came from the china works at the clay pits east of town. Mommy had a passion for strange and broken things, as long as they were clean, neatly presented and well arranged. Daddy sometimes complained about it, but not much.

It was his complaining that led me to knowing about where Daddy hid his work keys. They'd had one of their rare fights, and Mommy had said,

"It's no worse than your closet of glory, Jack Puca."

Then they'd both glanced at me, Daddy shamefaced and Mommy with a sly wink, and gone on to discuss other things.

Well, I knew there weren't any spare closets in the house. It wasn't like we had much spare of anything, unless you counted Cameron as a spare for me. So one time when Mommy and Daddy were both out, at a ward meeting I think, I looked in their room real good, until I found a trapdoor above their tiny clothes closet. The trap was hard to see in the boards of the ceiling but I'd been looking closely for just such a thing.

Once found, it wasn't difficult to open. I'd climbed up on top of Mommy's wool basket and chinned myself into the attic space.

I don't know why Mommy called it a closet of glory. It was pretty inglorious. First of all it was small. Daddy had to have bent over to fit up there, with the stuff that was already crowded in. I struck a match to light my candle and see what was at hand.

There was a saddle, like for a horse, though it took me a few moments to realize it wasn't just a badly-made footstool. The leather was old and cracked but it had silver chasing on it in long flowing lines that looked like leaves or narrow-bodied dragons. I bent and looked close. I couldn't see why we were so poor if Daddy had silver hidden away, but then I spotted where there had once been jewels on the saddle, pried out so that only tarnished little prongs remained.

I imagined him up here, stealing his own jewels one by one to stretch his pay packet on a cold winter's week. The thought hurt my heart. I looked around more.

A broken spear lay in three pieces against one corner of the tiny closet. There was big piece of cloth rolled up next to it. I touched that cloth -- silk. More stuff, too, a sort of sleeveless shirt of metal rings. It was armor like in the books of old stories. A sword with no grip, just a narrow tongue at the end of the blade. Had Daddy sold that grip off too at some point? A crown of leaves that when I touched them were metal, corroded to black. I rubbed some of the black off to find they were copper.

And junk. Lots of junk.

This wasn't glory. This was shame. He'd fought in the long-ago wars of our people, then laid down his arms to become a mill worker. What kind of man did that?

As I went to chin myself back down, I noticed that right by the trap door was a little pegboard with hooks. On one of the hooks hung Daddy's work keys.

It was to the closet of glory that I led Cameron that Saturday afternoon.

"Gee, your house is so nice *up here*," Cameron said. He was whispering, though.

"Don't track any dirt," I whispered back. At the door to Mommy and Daddy's room, I put my hand up. "Wait here. I'll get the keys."

"I'm coming, butt crack," Cameron hissed, and pushed me into Mommy and Daddy's room ahead of him.

Their bed was almost as high as my chest, with a quilt made from a lot of strange-colored scraps. It looked like autumn leaves to me sometimes, and sometimes like bloodstains from a secret murder. Two dressers, a lamp made from an old woman's shoe, and a little shelf with a few books. Plus more of Mommy's weird things.

There was an oval mirror and two pictures on the wall. One picture showed a desperate woman in a rowboat, a tapestry trailing into the water over the side. I chose to take that as a sign that we were doing the right thing in stealing Caliban's rowboat.

Borrowing, I corrected myself. We'd put it back when we were though.

The other picture showed a battle, men on horses with long spears and banners flying, flowing over a wall to meet an army with guns and cannon. We were losing. Even though it was only done in shades of gray, by someone who wasn't an expert hand with a pencil, that picture seemed to be a glimpse of a real moment in time.

Was that how Daddy's spear had broken?

It caught Cameron's eye, too, and he stopped to stare. I slipped open the closet door while he was looking at the wall and fished for the catch to the trapdoor. I didn't really want Cameron to know about Daddy's closet of glory—bad enough that my almost-brother was upstairs in the first place.

Not bad with me, I meant, but bad with Mommy and Daddy. If Cameron was okay, he wouldn't have been living in the basement.

I stopped, one hand brushing the edge of the opening above me. I'd never thought of it that way before. When I was little, I figured everybody had a brother in the basement. Later on, it was just the way things were.

Why *did* he live down there? Like a big rat or something.

Then I hopped up to grip the edge with one hand and reached around for the keys with the other. The effort made the muscles of my arm shiver.

"What you got up there, Henry?" Cameron asked. He startled me and I yelped, dropping to the ground to crush one of Mommy's hatboxes. The keys came with me, but there was a cracking sound above.

"Bones of god," I cursed — something I almost never did. Cameron was the privy mouth of the two of us.

He jumped up and chinned himself into the closet of glory.

"Get *out* of there," I almost shouted, tears of frustration standing in my eyes. There was no way I could hide that I'd been in the closet. Now I'd have to think of a really good story to explain why, and I was afraid I couldn't.

Cameron leaned over the opening to look down at me. His eyes and teeth seemed to gleam in the shadows above, which made him a monster version of me. "There's some cool crap up here. How come you never told me about this?"

"Because Daddy would kill us both and tan our hides for seat leather. We're already in deep doo-doo. Get back down here before you make it worse."

He stuck his tongue out at me, then dropped in a cloud of attic grime and his own special burnt stink of coal dust.

The closet was an unholy mess.

"We'd better clean up here," I said.

"Rowboat!" Cameron shouted, snatching Daddy's work keys out of my hand and sprinting for the front door.

It took me a moment to figure out that Cameron with the keys was worse trouble than the mess we'd already made, then I was after him.

Midsummer Avenue was the main street on the west side of town, where we lived tucked up against the bluff. It petered out south of Mabton to a gravel lane among orchards of hazelnuts, but in front of our house it was wide enough for mill busses, automobiles and horse carts to all pass each other at once. To the north it ran through downtown, where it acquired a double row of guardian cherry trees, then into the mill district before it ended at the gates of Caliban Products.

When he was feeling proud of his work Daddy liked to say the Puca family needed no other street. If Mommy was around, she would smile at him and remind him that the church was on Oak Street, and didn't we need that, and that his horrible little tavern was on Coal Street, and he seemed to need that as well against all common sense.

Right then Midsummer Avenue was the Puca family racecourse. Cameron was ahead of me by fifty feet or more. The keys jangled with every slamming step of his feet. I was mortified that I had to chase him down, scared that I wouldn't catch him, and terrified that someone would see him with that big ring of keys and somehow know what they were.

And more to the point, tell Daddy later.

I knew I couldn't catch my almost-brother by sheer speed. He was always a few steps faster and few punches stronger than me—had been all my life. But even on Saturdays Midsummer Avenue was busy—Cameron glanced back at me, grinning. I was watching for cross traffic, a turning truck or a horse cart pulling away from a delivery.

Cameron actually ran flat in to a brewery truck emerging from a side street as he looked over his shoulder. He bounced off like rubber ball to make a couple of feet of air before landing on his butt in the gutter. I sprinted and caught up just as he was back on his feet, tackling him to pull him down to the curb.

"Give me the keys right now," I said, "or it ends here."

"No boat?" He jangled the keys in front of me, keeping them just outside my reach. "You going to fly across the river, bro?"

"We're already *so* busted thanks to that mess you made back at the house. You want the rowboat, we do it my way."

Cameron laughed, his ape-grin on his face, and tossed me the keys. "Okay, little Daddy. Whatever you say."

"I say we walk like normal people. Don't draw no attention to ourselves. And see what's what when we get down to Caliban."

"Caliban, Caliban," Cameron chanted, "I just can't understand, what it is that any man, would hope to find at Caliban."

"And shut *up*," I told him.

Lady, he was annoying. I prayed that never in life would I act like my almost-brother.

Caliban Products stood before us, its ash-darkened stacks rising into the sky like three brick fingers echoing the magic of the Old Tower.

The mill was a complex really, spread out across a number of buildings, but it was all centered around the main plant and the powerhouse. The main plant was more than a quarter mile of brick, four or five stories high, though with only one level within—Daddy had given me a tour once, when the management had decided that a Family Day would be good press, he'd told me. Windows like fields of little square panes filled the walls of the main plant though most of the glass had been replaced with wood or cardboard or just painted over. Ornamented eaves hosted tribes of pigeons.

The powerhouse hulked by the river. Windowless as a prison, it gave an impression of bulky age though it was in fact one of the newest buildings. Daddy had explained to me that when the waterwheels were decommissioned and the great steam boilers brought in, Caliban had razed the old millhouse to its foundations, strengthened the brick and concrete courses where they anchored to the exposed rock of the riverbank, and built it all over again.

That was where we wanted to be. The boathouse would be tucked in to the foundations on the river side of the powerhouse.

I glanced around. We were before the main gate. Though no one seemed to be watching, it struck me as foolish to open that up and march right in. I knew there was a smaller gate to our left where the Caliban property met the Boott property. "Come on," I said to Cameron, and headed that way.

Inside the fence nothing moved. Railroad cars sat heavy and long on their rails, waiting to be drawn within the plant buildings or to carry coal to the powerhouse. Bricks and concrete stamped out any inch of nature that might have once existed. The buildings were all dark and age-grimed as the stacks.

It was like a great prison designed to confine the spirits of men and exclude all of nature.

No wonder Daddy went to drink with the railroad men.

We came to the little gate close by to where the walls joined. There was something carved in the stone arch over the door that I couldn't understand, even if hadn't been badly weathered. "LASCIATE OGEN SPERANZA," it read. Boott had a similar small gate just to the left that also opened onto the broken concrete of Midsummer Avenue's sidewalk. I imagined old man Caliban and old man Boott slinking out here on a stormy day to share cigarettes and plot their business, dividing competition and talking over which troublesome workers should not be further employed in Mabton.

Daddy had a lot of work keys and it took me a nerve-wracking time to find one that would fit the gate. The first I tried wasn't the right one and I had to keep working through different keys. I was afraid of being caught at any moment, a fear that multiplied whenever one of the occasional trucks grumbled past behind me.

The whole time Cameron chattered on about the liberating power of hard labor. As if he'd ever done any work in his life.

Finally we were inside Daddy's Caliban. We sprinted for the powerhouse though I knew that would mark us as troublemakers to anyone watching. Those banks of grimy windows had become too much like blank eyes to me, and for some reason I feared the ear-splitting shriek of a steam whistle.

All I heard besides the slap of my feet and the banging of my heart within my chest was Cameron laughing like one of the loons that came to the river in late autumn.

The boathouse was simple enough, a little shack between two piers of the powerhouse. I could see where the old axles of the mill wheels came out at the top of the foundation course. Before me were the brick shoulders of the now-broken dam that had once held Caliban's waters back. No need for the harness when the horse was gone.

Cameron applied himself to the boathouse lock, so I stared across the water. The river dropped through several stages of rapids or falls here. It was divided at the midpoint by a massive granite shoulder that was a smaller imitation of the bluff separating the bulk of Mabton from the water. That shoulder had allowed Caliban and Boott and the other mill builders to extend their will outward without actually touching the other bank and straying into the Lands of Promise with the dust of work upon them and cold iron in their hands.

I studied the ruined stones of the dams and the odd outcroppings of riverbed. Someone with determination and a good standing broad jump could make it out there, halfway across. Which made me wonder exactly what the river looked like on the other side of that big rock. Had the men who built the dams simply stopped there and turned their backs? Or had they looked onward with hope in their eyes?

Daddy might have been among them. Mommy had told me he'd worked at Caliban since the mill's founding sometime early in the last century. Proud as he was of being a shift supervisor, Daddy didn't talk about his history.

The closet of glory had shown me that.

"Got it," called Cameron behind me.

I turned to see the boathouse door open. He was already stepping into the shadows within. The lock lay upon the ground, hasp broken free from the old wood.

I could have cursed him for a boggart. We would be discovered *again*. I would be so deep in trouble there would never be another free day at Sunday market for me in my life.

There was nothing for it but to follow him.

The boathouse went far back into the foundations. There were racks like great wooden shelves empty of anything but dust. Cobwebbed ropes and chains hung. A tiny rowboat sat right behind the doors on a little sledge. Two oars stuck up from it like the skeleton of some very simple creature.

"*This* is going to take us across the river?" I couldn't keep the quaver from my voice.

"Solid as a rock," Cameron declared.

"Rocks don't float."

He grinned, grabbed an oar and banged it against the side of the boat. "See, tight and riverworthy."

"You knocked a hole in it," I pointed out, my heart sinking.

"Oh."

I sat down, exhausted. We'd stolen Daddy's keys, made a mess at the house and here at the mill. We were going to be caught, half a dozen times over, and in more trouble than I could imagine.

And I wasn't any closer to the Old Tower.

"Oars are good," Cameron said.

Oars.

Ropes.

All the things we'd wanted before but lacked.

"Grab them," I told him, feeling smarter than my almost-brother for once in my life. "Oars, and as much of the rope as we can carry that isn't already rotten."

"You building a raft again?" His voice was almost jeering.

"I'm going to *walk* across the river."

The late afternoon light had caught some of the golden glow of the far side of the river. The world was a jewel in amber. Milky white seeds soared on a wind that carried a scent of fresh-blooming flowers.

I stood on a boulder, watching the river drop fifteen or twenty feet just below me, and considered my next jump. Cameron waited two hops behind me with most of our load. He was within an easy rope toss if need be.

If there was ever a day when I would spread wings and fly like Ikarus of the Brass Islands, this was it. I could feel the call of the Old Tower pulling me ahead even as Caliban's sullen glower pushed me from behind.

In that moment, freed by water and the timeless light, I felt a profound sympathy for my father and all the long, pointless years of his life.

I sucked in my breath and leapt to land square on the wet boulder perhaps five feet ahead of me. With a shout of joy, I leapt to the next one, then the next, scrambling over the river and the remains of the dams in a bounding flight until I reached the granite wall at the center of river. There I stood panting and waited for my almost-brother.

He was not far behind, scuttling up with the ropes and the oars. "You can carry this stuff a while," Cameron announced. He tossed his load to the scrubby grass at our feet before laying down to rest.

I studied the far side of the granite. There was perhaps forty feet of channel between the cliff below me and the next jumble of rocks. From there it would be another series of hops to the shadowed willows where the fireflies already gleamed even though the westering day was still bright here in the middle of the river.

My heart ached to be across. I would find a way to be on the other side if I had to make the leap from where I stood.

But what a mighty leap that would be. Close to our right on the downstream side was a single fall that accounted for all the distance of the little jumps and rapids and cataracts on the mill side of the river in one great tumbling roar of water that vanished over the edge in rock-filled spray.

I paced the granite shoulder to the south end, upstream farthest away from the pull of the waterfall. It tapered there to a little gravel beach where tiny fish darted among the shallows. The channel was a bit wider at this end. Looking back up the granite slope to where Cameron lay, I saw dozens of cracks and fissures in the old rock.

Oars and rope. I smiled and headed back for Cameron's abandoned load.

Of course he followed me down the second time, chattering the whole way. "No boat, no wings, no magic boots. He's going to sail a rope across the river, our Henry is. You're nuts, bro. When we go home, I'm switching with you. You can sweat out your nights to the clanging of the furnace while I sit at the table upstairs. Because I'm the one who can appreciate it. Not you, no, you're the nutter who thinks he's a nixie or something."

He went on like that. I ignored him as I shoved one of the oars deep as it would go into a crack near the south end of the granite. Then I tied off the longest rope we'd salvaged and walked it back up the hill to estimate its length.

Not enough.

Another rope, then, and double-hitch them together. I worked at that a moment as my almost-brother's voice ran down. Stripped my clothes and shoes off and rigged a third rope for a sling around me. Fastened the second rope and my clothing bundle to it. Finally I looked up at him.

Cameron was grinning his ape-grin again. "I'm proud of you, Henry."

"Thanks." I was suddenly struck shy.

"When you drown, can I have your room?"

"I am epoptic," I told him. "The Lady carries me in Her hands." Then: "Hang on to this end of the rope. When I get across, I'll tie down the other end so you can follow."

He hugged me, quick and rough. "I have always loved you."

I thought no more upon it. Instead I jumped into the river, which was shocking cold and tasted of the coming evening. Arms wrapped around the paddle, I kicked into the current making for the other side. I would not let the falls just downstream concern me.

I had read the books of old stories, of the Bright Days when our people in their glory and their ignorance rode from the Garden Beneath like a storm upon the earth. To me, those stories all had a single point: that the banners were more brilliant, the sword-edges sharper, the loves truer in those old times than any tired modern imitation could be in our world of clocks and hunting licenses and pay packets.

I didn't know about that. I was a boy, sharing my childhood with Cameron in a town among a people who have few children in their long years. Daddy or old Mrs. Grimsby might have slain gods when they were young, but now we all shopped at Diana's Market and rode the bus out to the Town Fair on Midsummer's Day.

But one thing I know from the old stories. There are moments in life when the Lady stays time's hand and people can see the map of their existence unfolded, all their choices written out in a glowing script.

The river gave me one of those moments.

It was cold, cold as iron in the night. It had a fist that gripped my chest tight as I'd squeezed any frog I'd ever caught. My ribs ached in the first moment. My lungs burned though my head remained above the water. My entire body echoed to the rumble of the falls. That tumbling water called to me with a voice almost as powerful as that of the river's other side.

I could have let go, slipped my knots, and slid smiling over the precipice into sharp-edged chaos. Only the wonder of that glint high in the Old Tower kept me going at that moment.

Then my purpose reasserted itself and I began to swim in earnest. Rope or no rope this was a perilous crossing. I kept the second oar clutched to my chest as both float and cargo and kicked as hard as if I were fighting Cameron over the last scrap of some sweetmeat. Harder, really, for though he sometimes seemed to have no limits to his ferocity, I never really meant to hurt my almost-brother.

The rope was long enough to let me reach the other side. It was short enough to hold me back from the falls should my strength fail in the cold dark water. But only if the knots held and the oar remained true where I had grounded it in the crevice. Only if Cameron watched over me.

Still, mere seconds had gone by as I thought over my choices and fates. I kicked again. The river was like Mommy, bigger than I could imagine, but close to me every moment. The river was like Daddy, a cold and distant power that drove my life. The river was like Cameron, worrying at my heels to make me stronger and better than I would have become on my own.

The rope jerked then. Cameron? I could not turn to look. He would haul me back if he needed to. I continued to kick.

The cold was getting worse, a wintry iron straining the muscles of my legs and lungs. I had considered the distance and difficulty of the swim but not the temperature. The Old Tower still called me.

Why did Mommy keep warning me away from it? I would no more have thought to cross the river on my own than I would have thought to fly to the moon.

Daddy never spoke of it. Kicking again, I realized Mommy had never spoken of it in Daddy's presence, either.

The rope jerked another time. Not hard, though. That must be Cameron paying the line out. The falls continued to rumble in my bones. My fingers and toes were numb. I wondered if I should have kept my clothes on.

Kick.

Why had no one ever gone to the Old Tower? Daddy and a handful of his drinking partners could have found a way across this channel.

Kick.

Even my thoughts were slowing. The falls called to me in voices of wonder, promising rest. My arms and legs were wood. Lead. Stone.

Kick.

I knew why we had left the Garden Beneath. It was not large enough for our people's honor and glory. The apes had been spreading across the world building villages and temples of their own. We had meant to show them a thing or two.

Kick.

Now we were no different from them.

Another tug upon the rope.

Kick.

My legs were slower. The falls were louder. The Lands of Promise were close. All I had to do was slip the knots.

Kick.

My fingers fumbled at my chest, but the wet ropes defeated them. I found it hard to hold the oar and do that, so I let it go.

Kick.

Where was Cameron, when he should be rescuing me?

Kick.

I began to tumble, nearly in the grip of the falls. Then I hit a rock, bounced off another rock with a bruising jolt to my shoulder. I struck a third with my jaw so that blood bloomed in my mouth.

My hands grabbed on without further thought. Something tugged at my back like the bite of a fish, then my foot found another rock.

I pulled myself upward, spitting water and blood, until I was wedged above the river though still in the freezing spray. I rubbed sweat and my eyes and looked across the channel.

Cameron stood there hugging Daddy. Another man was close by with a rifle raised to his shoulder. His head was wreathed in smoke.

My father glared at me above my almost-brother's shoulder.

I scrambled up and away as rock chips flew. I heard no shot, but the falls overwhelmed my ears. My foot caught in a cleft, skin scraping to the bone as I pulled it free, but I kept going. Something plucked at my ear, then the rock in front of me exploded. I closed my eyes and kept on climbing, over the top of a boulder and out of sight of the other side of the river.

No, my side of the river.

I was on the other side now.

Back against the rock, coughing up water and blood, I waited for my lungs to work again. When they finally did, I picked at the knots of my rope until my clothes came free, and dressed in the freezing garments. Then I worked my way across the rest of the river for the safety of the willows, away from bullets and not-brothers and un-Daddys and whatever had gone wrong at home.

I slept weeping that night high in a willow tree set back from the bank. Noises echoed from across the river, booms and bellowings and something much like Mommy's voice except far too large and deep in volume. My cold and my fear combined to an exhaustion that ignored all else.

Looking through the willow leaves into the orange glare of the rising sun, Daddy's Caliban was a castle of the Bright Days. The smoke-grimed stacks were towers set to challenge the armies of the Earth.

Then I woke a little more and saw only cold iron and failure.

At least no one stood on that granite rock in the middle of the river with rifle in hand.

My entire body ached. My head split with the pain of a river-cold. My nose ran and my eyes were swollen. If this was the Land of Promises, the Lady had lied to us.

I smiled at the thought. What would Mother Arleigh say to me now?

"Get out of that tree, you little ape," most likely.

So I climbed to the ground. I had to be two or three miles north of the Old Tower, and considerably down hill. Battered and chilled, with no paths through these woods, it would take me most of the morning to reach it.

"Mommy," I told the indifferent midges that swarmed the riverbank, "I am going where you sent me."

Around noon I walked slowly uphill through the golden fields that I had always been able to see from the top of the bluff. There were no pale stags today. Only the sun's welcome heat and the cycling buzz of the grasshoppers. The slope stole my energy and gave back only a deep stitch in my side, so I took my rest on a tumbled stone.

As I sat I turned to look across the river. Seen from this side, the bluff was a steep-kneed cliff topped with the rhododendrons and scraggled copse of woods I knew so well. There were caves in the face of the cliff, which surprised me. It had never occurred to me such openings might be down there. Did they connect anywhere in the town?

I watched a while. Things moved in the cave shadows. I even glimpsed a glint, an echo of what had finally drawn me to the Old Tower. Binoculars? A camera, maybe.

I began to wave when another thought occurred to me   That glint might be the sight of a hunting rifle.

They were watching me. Had they always been watching me?

That ended my rest. I kept walking, zigging across the fields both to lessen the slope and to make myself harder to see from Mabton.

As I climbed the Old Tower rose above me like a thin stone moon. This close I could see that it was built from huge stones much bigger than any single man could lift. Some had shifted or cracked, which lent the Old Tower its distinctive angle.

But it was definitely *built*. It was by far the oldest thing I had ever seen.

Except, I realized, for Mrs. Grimsby. And anyone else in Mabton who could remember the Garden Beneath from their own lifetime.

That made me understand how little my life meant to those people. I was no more than a swamp midge to Mrs. Grimsby, or Mother Arleigh, or even Daddy. To anyone who'd ridden under the brilliant banners of the Bright Days, whether or not they remembered the Garden Beneath.

Only Cameron understood me. And he had betrayed me to Daddy.

I stopped just outside the Old Tower. Was this what the Lady had promised us? Had we earned the Lands of Promise?

And who was I to the Lady anyway?

Builder of bridges, perhaps.

I laughed at myself. These were grand dreams for someone who had been the target of bullets.

I stepped through the high, narrow door into cold shadows.

The Old Tower didn't really have stairs. More like climbing blocks set into the wall in a rough spiral. There was a stone floor with a narrow gap like a grave leading downward. The interior of the tower stretched above me, a chimney to a ceiling perhaps forty feet high. There was no sign within of anyone who had ever lived here or held this tower against their enemies.

It might as well have been a cave.

Something gleamed in the gap at my feet. I stepped around to look down a narrow stone stair. A ghostly bluish light shimmered in the dank dark. It was the exact shade of the spark which had passed between me and Cameron.

I squinted. What was I seeing? Armor, maybe. Like grave goods.

Or Daddy's closet of glory.

There were swords there, too, with their own light. Had this been the glint I had seen from the tower walls, some glimpse of martial glory? My blood stirred. The war horns would be brassy and proud. This time we would have guns, too, for we had come to abide the feel of cold iron all too well.

But I was tired and chilled, with no stomach for the darkness beneath the earth. This crypt could not have gleamed to me from across the river, I, realized. So I headed for Father Sun instead. As I climbed the tower wall I found that my arms and legs ached from the river. My ears rang, either from my river-cold, or from the close call of the shooting. My breath hurt. But I still climbed, knowing I would find something. Something had glinted from this tower. Something had held Mommy's attention and my imagination all my life.

After a while I came to the ceiling. There was a narrow crack in the capstone which blocked the tower shaft. Sunlight glared through it like a mirror of the grave of glory at the base. I squeezed through, picking up a few more scrapes along the way.

Above was like the battlement of a castle in an old story. There was a wall, varying from knee-high to chest-high in random order as the shapes of the stones dictated. But there was nothing here, either. No glint or goddess or voice out of history.

I leaned against the wall facing the sun and cried for a little while out of frustration.

"I am epoptic," I told the sky, then took a nap in the warm sunlight.

Later when I awoke I stood stiff but clear-headed and looked back across the river. The Old Tower was higher than the bluff. I could actually see some of Mabton beyond, as well as the mills downstream to the north. The sun was heading west, already behind me and again the day was filled with long, golden light. The fields and farms east of Mabton seemed enchanted. The ribbon of the railroad headed through them like a highway back to the Bright Days.

Closer to me, the river's edge below the bluffs seemed as mysterious and filled with portent as this side ever had when viewed from over there. The mills almost glowed in the amber light.

Our people have purpose.

The thought surfaced in me like a leaping fish. We no longer die on sword's point. We don't fight wars with the apes or duels with each other. We heed steam whistles and go to church and drink ourselves silly and buy peanut butter at the Sunday market and live out the long days of our lives in something like peace and harmony.

It is the small miracles of kitchen and paycheck that are our Lands of Promise. Not the war horns and bright banners, nor the endless plenty of some mythic paradise.

"Thank you, Lady," I said. I understood Her purpose now, and Her promise as well. I climbed down before daylight fled the tower.

At the bottom, where dusk already gathered among the cold stones, I looked once more into the gap that led to earth below. That blue glow still flickered. It was Oberon's vault, a closet of glory for our entire people. There would be weapons and relics below to stir our people to a revival of the Bright Days once more, however brief and doomed that might be.

Again I could hear the war horns blaring. Had I come here by night I might have first followed that glow down in the earth. I would have missed the Lady's message waiting for me above.

Or perhaps She had prepared more than one message for me.

Did the Lady care which direction her people followed? Or only that we followed some direction.

Outside, Cameron sat on a tumbled stone eating an apple.

I couldn't find it in me to be surprised. "Have you come to kill me?"

He took a huge bite, juice streaming sticky down his chin. After he'd chewed and swallowed Cameron grinned his ape grin. "They think you're me, now. I told Daddy I'd gone crazy, and you'd pushed me into the river."

I? You? "And he brought a rifleman out there just for that."

Cameron shrugged. "He didn't know it was us who'd broken into the mill."

"So what are you doing here now?"

His eyes glinted like stars. "Maybe I'm lying. But not all of time. Not everything I say. Truth, Henry. There's some folks mighty worried about what you might have found or raised over here. Like old man Caliban. Other folks, like Mommy, well...she's sort of holding back the tide right now."

"The caves in the cliff?"

He shrugged again. "Rich people want things, too. All their money can't buy their way into the Lands of Promise. You're the first person to cross the river alive."

"What about you?"

Cameron leaned in close, so that I could smell apple and onions and coal dust. "We're the same person, Henry. Only Mommy ever saw us different. Only Mommy made us different."

The hair on my neck prickled. I remembered her greatness, that vast presence I saw out of the corner of my eye. "You're lying again," I said, but I didn't believe myself.

He shrugged, then dropped the half-eaten apple into his pocket. My almost-brother — perhaps my almost-self — led me down to the river bank where a little boat was wedged into a marshy shallow. He might have come across on it. If he had, he'd made it seem as if the boat had drifted in.

We both got on board. I took the oars to row across. On the way we talked about church and school and the Sunday market and which kind of candy was best at Pinfaire's Emporium. The current caught the boat and pulled it, but I stayed firm on the oars.

When the boat ground into rocks just above Boott's Mill, I was alone. I couldn't remember exactly when Cameron had left. I hadn't heard a splash. A half-eaten apple sat on the boat's other bench. When I picked it up, a blue spark jumped from the apple to me.

My brother had come home.

Then men with guns met me there, and a constable, and Peggy's father the judge, along with Daddy and Mommy both.

"Well," said Daddy in his roughest, you're-going-to-get-a-whipping voice.

"I have seen the Lands of Promise," I answered loudly, so that everyone could hear. Some of the guns clicked as they were cocked. "We are living in them even now, on this side of the river."

In the end, no one believed me but Mommy. They all argued a while, for years in fact, but no one else seemed tempted to cross the river to see for themselves.

One night a month or so after I'd returned from the other side, Mommy showed me Her fullness, by way of a parting gift — or perhaps a terror. "I have given you back all of yourself," She told me in a voice like mountains groaning. "I am sorry that I cannot give you back to your mother, too." Then the Lady kissed me and was gone on the autumn wind.

I still see blue sparks among the leaves sometimes in that season, and hints of the banners that would have flown again had I gone down into the earth below the Old Tower. When the leaves burn in piles, I know what would have become of those banners. Just like the picture on the wall of Daddy's room.

Peggy likes me these days. Maybe we'll be together and have a kid of our own sometime in the next century or two. Old man Caliban told Daddy I could have a job in security down at the mill when I finish school. When our paths cross Mother Arleigh looks at me with a faraway sadness in her eyes. Since Mommy left, she and Daddy drink together down at the Switchman's Rest on Sundays, though they try to hide that from me.

Someday when I am very, very old and all my life's secrets are long past mattering, I will tell Mother Arleigh that I know who she really is and that I love her too.

the river knows its own

The Willamette Valley woods were filled with that old magic of childhood. His thoughts suspended somewhere between dreams and memories, Jorge walked among the bright-speckled shadows like spilled coins, stepped over mossy logs with long green fingers, scrambled down stony creek beds that could have been fortress walls a hundred generations past. Early autumn in Oregon was brisk without chill, sunny without warmth — an intermediate season, as if all the Earth were held in balance.

That was the day Jorge saw the dragon.

It rustled among the trees, moving against the wind. He glanced toward the sound expecting to see a deer. Instead there was flash of dark-veined brown, like world's largest maple leaf gone half-rotten, accompanied by a smell to match, borne on a gust of air colder than a Mt. Hood glacier.

Jorge stopped. His boots squelched as they sank ankle-deep in mud the color of fresh cow manure. He stared across the banks of mist-spotted ferns that covered the ground between the boles of the trees.

What had he really seen?

Then a raven screeched in the hawthorn branches overhead. Distracted by the noise, Jorge slipped and landed on his hands and butt in mud. He pulled himself out and tried to remember why he had stopped. Shaking the cobwebs from his mind, he continued his hike.

Two days later, Jorge sat outside It's A Beautiful Pizza on SE Belmont Street nursing a tall iced chai. He hadn't felt the same since he came back from his hiking trip. After a few hours of futzing around at work that morning Venera had told him to get out, take the day, and find his damned head.

Given the shoestring their little water quality nonprofit ran on, she had been mighty generous with his time. That was typical of Venera. His boss was something of a witch chick with her purple skirts and weird silver charms, but she almost always knew what she was about. It was one the many things he really dug about her, though he'd never quite had the nerve to put a move on to match his feelings.

Old Volvos in need of valve jobs clattered past, interspersed with VW Vanagons, ancient Dodges, and all the other stereotypically unique vehicles driven by the tragically hip and hopelessly hippie types that haunted Belmont. "If you believed your own shit, you'd ride the bus," he told the traffic.

As ever, the cars didn't listen. No one listened. That was only one of the world's many problems. Getting close to Venera was one of his.

"Hey," said a woman. "Didn't you hear me?"

Jorge looked up, half hiding behind his chai cup. She was a skinny white chick with a shoe leather tan and wind-burned cheeks, muscled arms like knotted ropes, and a macramé vest that didn't show much chest. Her hair was dark brown matted dreads that almost matched the brown of her eyes. She wore a pair of faded jeans covered in ballpoint doodles that were either high art, deep social commentary or disguises for the stains.

The kind of chick Portland was full of. The kind of chick he liked.

A chick he didn't know.

Thoughts of Venera blew out of his head like mist on a sunny day.

"No," Jorge said slowly. "I'm sorry. I didn't hear you."

Then she laughed. In that moment she transformed from earthy-attractive to heart-stoppingly beautiful, with no more than a few loud breaths and a flash of teeth like white corn. "That's okay, I didn't say nothing. I was just wondering if you heard me."

"Sit," said Jorge from the depths of love-struck awe. "Please." He waved his chai at the plastic chair on the other side of the tiny table.

Sit she did, and took his chai right out of his hand. After a long, slow slurp she smiled again, this time without the laugh. "I don't know how you can stand this stuff." She took another long slurp.

"Are we having the same conversation?"

She cocked her head, a brown bird on a green chair. "We could be. I didn't think you were the type."

"I'm not." He was ready to be whatever type she wanted. He wished like hell he'd worn his Guatemalan vest that morning.

"You're whatever type I want, right?"

Her words jarred. How had she known? "Ah..." he ventured.

"I can read the signs. Any girl does. Any girl that wants to make it in the world without a McHouse and three kids for shining armor." The smile again. She set the chai down on the little table. "But somebody told me about you."

Another slip of the mental gears. He reached for the cup, for something to do, and to feel the transient warmth of her hand. "Who?" he asked before taking a sip.

The chai now tasted old, stale, like rotten leaves and the smell of cold rock on the face of the mountain. Bending forward he spit it out, swallowed a curse, then wiped his hand across his lips and looked up to apologize.

No one was there. The sidewalk was empty. A crow screeched like a rusty hinge as two Volvos banged bumpers and Jorge suddenly wondered why he wasn't at work. Venera would be missing him.

"Something's fucked up, man," Jorge said. He sipped on a fuzzy navel which he then set down in front of him next to some peanuts in one of those little parquet-looking salad bowls from the 1970s. Buzzing beer signs cast murky multicolored shadows across the bar top like a slow motion disco show. Silent televisions flickered through Keno, ESPN and an old Tom Cruise movie. It was the Bear Paw on a Monday night.

Clark the bartender grunted. "Something's always fucked up. Wouldn't be having this job otherwise." He drew off a pint of the latest Widmer seasonal ale for someone back at the pool tables. Clark was a huge black man, with a flaming wheel tattooed on his bald scalp, right pinkie finger missing. He wore a blue muscle shirt and those long-legged basketball shorts in red-and-blue Kansas Jayhawk colors.

"No, no, you don't get it." But Clark was gone, and for a moment that scared Jorge. Things kept disappearing, he didn't know what—or worse, who—only that they were gone.

Clark came right back, though, which eased Jorge's mind. The bartender reached for the remains of the fuzzy navel, but Jorge waved him off.

"Maybe you've had enough, friend," the bartender said.

"That ain't it."

Bar towels snapped for a moment as Clark busied himself. Then the big man chuckled. "I ain't getting out of this, am I? Tell old Clark."

"Stuff keeps disappearing."

"You sound like my Momma. She got the Alzheimer's. Thinks people steal her underwear at night." Clark chuckled without any humor. "While she's wearing it."

Jorge felt a cold tightness in his scalp. "I don't know, man. It's like I *am* crazy."

"Mm..."

"In the woods." He drained the last of the fuzzy navel. Leaves swirled in memory. "Muddy trail, I stopped. There was something, but I can't remember what. Like it left a hole in my head."

Clark frowned. "You fell down and hit your head? Go see a doctor."

"No, no. I mean, I wound up on my ass, but not like that. Then the next day, something happened to my chai."

"Something happened to your chai?" Clark flicked a bar towel at him. "You *do* be fucked up, friend."

"That's what I'm trying to tell you."

Then a big guy, seven feet at least, covered in hair and not much else, shambled in through the padded door and took the stool next to Jorge. That was when he *knew* he was crazy.

"Try again," rumbled the big guy in a voice like rocks falling in a canyon.

"Try what?" whispered Jorge. He glanced at Clark. The bartender was dropping onion rings in the fryer and not noticing anything. I will not forget this time, Jorge thought. He began to draw a crude sketch of the newcomer on his bar napkin.

"Hard to talk."

"Hard to fucking remember." Jorge immediately wished he hadn't said it that way. This was a time to be polite.

"Hard to be," said the Sasquatch.

And it *was* a Sasquatch. Jorge was certain. "What's hard to be?"

"Listen." One massive paw pinned his writing hand to the bar. Jorge could feel the pen barrel snap as cool ink flooded across his skin. "Things move. Things change. The stones are being called to dance."

He had that wrong party feeling again. "I don't know—"

The Sasquatch interrupted. "River man. Tree man. Land man. You can listen, know. The stones dance, the waters spread. The west flies."

Jorge's temper welled up. "For Christ's sake, talk some fucking sense."

Clark turned around. "What?"

Alone at the bar, Jorge looked at his ink-stained hand. This time he remembered. Some. Love, fear, a hairy monster spouting cryptic wisdom.

It didn't make a hell of a lot of sense, but it was *memory*. And there were words soaking into his skin, written in a crabbed script that looked like no alphabet he knew.

"What the hell's the matter with you?" Clark asked as he realized what the ink mess on the bar top was. "I'm cutting you off, Georgie-boy."

"It's not..." Jorge stopped. He flipped a twenty on the dry part of the bar—more than he could afford, but he didn't want Clark mad at him. Jorge had to live in this neighborhood. "I'm sorry. I told you man, I'm a little fucked up today."

Clark grunted something and made the bill disappear. Jorge was whistling when he banged his way out the padded door. Venera would help him. She was a mystic *witchy* chick. He'd never believed that shit, but this disappearing memory stuff was right up his boss's alley.

There was just one question. Who had he fallen in love with? It had been something different than his low-level hots for Venera.

Not the Sasquatch, surely.

There was fire in the sky above Wye-east mtn. last night after I kilt the she-baer. I tole Whiskey Jack we shood ott to of asked them Clakkamas about the she-bear but he larfed and spit at me. We watched that fire shoot up sparks and flame and clouds whitch glowed like a Chinee lanthorn. A while after Whiskey Jack passed on to snoring I spied wings in the fire. It were a lizzard bigger than all of St. Louie I swear on my Bible. Today Whis. Jack tells me I am plumb crazy. But I am go-ing to find me them Clakkamas injuns and ask about the lizzard.

-- Journal of Oregon country frontiersman Marc Beaulieu, undated, ca. 1793-1795

Jorge banged on the door of Venera's apartment. She had to be home. Monday night wasn't one of her date nights as far as he knew from office chat. Such as it was. She was very private about her life outside work.

He kept track of that dating stuff anyway. Just in case.

Light gleaming through the blinds just to his left threw thin lines on the damp concrete of the third-floor balcony. He'd never actually been inside, just picked her up for carpools to state Watershed Enhancement Board meetings and stuff. He cupped his hands to his mouth and pressed against the window. "You home?" he shouted.

The cheap aluminum frame distorted his words into a sort of industrial echo of himself.

There was no answer, but he heard thumping. Then the door was yanked open. Venera stood there wild-eyed and angry. She was African-American, head shaved, with skin darker than espresso, well over six feet and built like a mechanical pencil. Right then she wore a pair of panties a few threads away from being a thong and a torn t-shirt that was inside out and backwards.

Jorge's pulse shot up and his mouth went dry.

"What the—" Venera shouted, then stopped. Her eyes narrowed as she studied Jorge. "You still ain't found your damned head, have you?" Though her voice was softer, she wasn't smiling.

An unsmiling Venera was often a bad thing.

He found his voice. "No, I haven't found it. But I know what happened." Sort of.

"And this involves me *how*?"

He showed her the markings on his right hand, words written spontaneously in ink.

"Ah." She stared at his hand a moment. "I see," she finally said. "Wait here." Then Venera slammed the door.

Jorge leaned against the jamb for a little while, trying to look like he wasn't a drug buyer waiting on a score. Voices rose and fell with the rhythms of argument somewhere inside Venera's apartment.

Oops.

It *was* date night. No wonder she'd been pissed. Now he wished he'd stopped at the Plaid and grabbed a six of microbrew or something. It was too late, though—he couldn't be gone when she next opened the door.

Besides, he really wanted to see what kind of person it took to score with her.

Twenty minutes later Jorge wished he'd headed for the c-store after all. He'd gone so far as to drag out his car keys, but hadn't worked up the nerve to leave after bothering Venera. The letters on his hand were starting to look blurry—sweat?—and his memories which had seemed so clear, if confused, when leaving the bar were vanishing like a nitrous buzz.

He should go home and take a long, hot shower.

Then the door banged open again. Different woman this time, heavy chick not much over five feet tall with a sort of Filipina/blended-race look and Frieda Kahlo eyebrows. She had on a tattered Howard the Duck babydoll worn to translucency by too many spin cycles, and not much else—massive dark nipples showed through like a pair of bruised eyes.

That explained a lot, he realized. Why Venera never seemed to vibe off him the way he vibed off her.

"You know," the woman said, "I don't get out much." She grinned at him, nasty and irritated. "Even when I do, I don't get a lot of nookie." A pudgy finger tapped his chest. "So skinny-butt Mediterranean hunks bothering my girlfriend piss me off. Now let me see your hand."

Jorge offered his ink-stains. She grabbed him hard on the wrist like his grandmother used to do, then spread his fingers. Front, back, she flipped the hand. Back, front. She even sighted down his fingertips as if they were arrows. Or gun barrels.

He was really starting to wish he'd just gone home. This was embarrassing.

"Where?" she asked. Her expression wasn't as hard now.

"Bear Paw over on Milwaukie, near the Aladdin."

"Some guy just attack you with a biro?"

"No...it was..." Jorge glanced around. He didn't want anyone listening in. The story was too weird. He leaned forward and whispered. "Sasquatch."

"Sasquatch?" Her face went sour, like she'd eaten a bad malted milk ball. Or was talking to an idiot. "Bigfoot? Hairy pecker, about so tall?" She reached up as far as her arm would go, setting Howard's tattered cigar bobbing on her shirtfront.

"Taller, I think," he said, trying to keep his eyes on her face.

"And you're not drunk." It was a statement. "Better come in." She turned and walked into the apartment, trusting him to follow. "Hey, V, the Lansquenet's going to be pissed!"

A few minutes later the three of them sat around a dinette table that boasted a ridged aluminum edge and a formica top in foam green with those little boomerang thingies running in a pattern all over. The rest of the apartment was decorated to match the table—faux-Fifties Portland kitsch mixed with metrosexual modern. The table was covered in roach burns, Chinese takeout wrappers, beer bottles and, now, Jorge's forearms.

He was very tired, but Venera's girlfriend insisted on copying the smudged letters or patterns or whatever they were on his right hand. She wasn't doing what he would have done—trying to reproduce them in lines of text—but rather executing a more-than-competent life drawing of his hand and illustrating the ink stains in place.

Venera touched Jorge's chin with her long, cool fingers. That gave him a little shiver on the spine, and he found himself wishing she meant it. After a moment her fingers trailed around his face before dropping to his shoulder, then away. Already he missed their faint pressure.

"What?" Jorge asked. He felt bleary, almost drugged.

"You ain't right, Jorge, and you ain't getting any righter. Can you remember what the hairy man said to you?

He wanted to say, *touch me again, please.* Instead: "He was going on about rivers and trees and stuff. How I'd understand. Then he said..." Forgetting her fingers, Jorge reached for the words. "He said, 'The stones dance, the waters spread. The west flies.' And when he talked, I remembered other stuff."

"Yeah?"

"A dragon on the wing in the woods. A beautiful girl who wasn't there."

Venera got her smile back. That made him shiver again.

"How'd you nail down your memory of the hairy man?" asked Venera's girlfriend.

"Drew him on a napkin."

The two women exchanged a glance. "Like a Scriptor," said Venera.

Her friend nodded. "You want to summon the Five?" she asked. "He's Coloring up good. A wild Skill maybe."

Venera looked thoughtful. "I'm thinking of calling Aristides instead. Back in New York."

"I know where he is."

"Well, this is his kind of thing."

"Don't you go calling him up, girl. That man is not your friend, and he sure ain't mine. You don't want the Five, we'll work this through ourselves." Then, almost grudgingly to Jorge, "Good work, skinny butt. Not a lot folks would think to do that. Even them that should know better."

"I think he *wanted* me to remember," said Jorge, who was no longer making any sense of the conversation. His ears were cold. The tabletop rushed up to meet his face.

Jorge woke up flat on his back to a pressure on his chest that made him gasp for air. He looked up into the pendulous naked breasts of Venera's girlfriend. She was straddling his belly, eyes closed, singing.

He, on the other hand, was fully clothed. Besides the view, there didn't seem to be much in this for him. And she was *Venera's* girlfriend.

In some dreams maybe, but not this one. "Um, hey, this, uh..."

Something whacked the top of his head and Venera hissed, "Quiet, fool."

So he was quiet.

The girlfriend kept singing. It was tuneless chant that didn't stick on any tempo or key, but seemed to wander like a spring breeze. Her head swung back and forth as she sang—as if she were listening, too.

After a while she grabbed his inked right hand and pressed it between her breasts. Jorge felt his face grow hot while his penis seemed to crinkle tight and small in a sort of anti-erection. Then she opened her eyes. He would have sworn they were glowing.

"Things move." Her voice was a strange, squeaky echo of the hairy man's. "Things change. The stones are dancing, the waters are spreading. The west flies."

"Why me?" he asked.

"You do watershed conservation work," said Venera, still out of his sight line though he tried to roll his eyes back far enough to find her. Her burred voice was softer than he could remember ever hearing it. "And you walk the land. You don't just stare at hydrology reports and doodle on maps like some office dork. The land *knows* you, Jorge."

The girlfriend dropped his hand and leaned so close that her breasts nudged his chin. "There's Skilled been working forty years in the Lansquenet that don't have your kind of grounding, skinny butt. You ain't gonna be popular."

"Skilled," said Jorge. Trying not to look at her tits was making him cross-eyed. "Lands-canay. Dancing stones. Whatever. Look, I came over here because Venera's witchy and this felt like witchy business." He tried to nod, indicate his unseen boss somewhere behind him. This was definitely not the evening of his fantasies. "Been hanging around you too long, V. I think I'm going to go sleep this off."

The girlfriend got up off him, moving fast and spry for such a heavy woman. "Lost that option when you bound the hairy man to your memory. Now you can't walk away."

Jorge staggered to his feet. "No, I'm going home. Slam a double shot, drop a few aspirin, sleep twelve hours, it'll be like none of this ever happened."

Venera caught his eye. "I can't stop you, but that's a bad move."

He shrugged. He could start looking for another job in a couple of days. Way this was going, he'd have to. Maybe then she'd let him take her out. "I don't believe this shit anyway."

"It don't matter what you believe. The land is real with or without you."

The girlfriend finished shrugging back into her Howard the Duck top. "Next time, skinny butt, we both get naked." She winked. "More power, more fun."

Now he had an erection. Jorge stepped as quickly out the door as his dignity would allow, then trotted stiff-legged for the car. He wondered if Clark would serve him any more tonight.

All the way home, the ink on his hand itched as fiercely as any paper cut. It felt blood-warm.

He rode the Filipina witch from behind, her broad sweat-slicked buttocks pressed up against his pelvis as his cock split her vagina like a pomegranate. She pushed and tossed, growling so deep he could feel the rumbling where their bodies met. The room wasn't clear to him—an enormous black space with distant, shadowy pillars—but the sheen of perspiration on her skin was cake icing.

Jorge pulled out slick and hard, ready to cornhole her. As he slid in into the rubbery fist-grip of her anus, she turned to look at him, but it was the hairy man from the bar who grinned. The sweet, salty icing on her back turned to his fuzz. Jorge didn't usually play that way, but he was too far into the sex to stop. As he pounded against the hairy man's ass he realized that his partner's back was tattooed with a map of the Willamette Valley, from the Columbia River along his shoulders—complete with a red-orange splotch at the top for Mt. St. Helens—on down to Grant's Pass where Jorge continued to thrust.

Mt. Hood sat below the tattoo of Bonneville Dam on hairy man's right shoulder blade, the volcano an orange glare much brighter than St. Helens. Jorge found himself staring into an eye at the center of the mountain's tattoo, a glossy, angry eye that returned his look. The eye tracked his gaze as he bucked and thrust. The hairy man began to shake with his orgasm, an earthquake rocking the valley, until Jorge was thrown off into a screaming freefall high above the textured white mountaintops that ended tangled in his sticky sheets.

Pyroclastic flows are high-speed avalanches of hot rock, gas, and ash that are formed by the collapse of lava domes or eruption columns. They can move up to 100 miles per hour and have temperatures to 1500° F. They are lethal, burning, burying, or asphyxiating all in their paths.
— United States Geological Survey Fact Sheet 060-00

Morning brought a watercolor sky and that kind of Oregon rain that was basically aggressive mist. Jorge drowsed facing the window and wondering at how humid his bedroom seemed to be. His eyes and mouth felt gritty while his entire body ached as if the fall—

That thought brought him bolt awake in remembered panic. His clock was blinking, reset by some electrical failure in the night, but that much light outside meant he was late for work. And his bed...his bed...

Jorge was surrounded by half-rotted leaves, pine needles, rich loam. He was lying in it, like a man dragged from a shallow grave on the forest floor.

The grit on his face was soil. His nails were stained brown with the stuff.

"Holy crap!" he shouted. Somehow Venera's girlfriend *had* gotten in here last night. The two witchy-women were fucking with him. In all the wrong ways.

He picked his way through a litter of sticks and bark to the bathroom. He would wash the dirt and grime off, get to work, and have it out with Venera. There were other jobs, damn it. Other women, for that matter. This creepy shit about breaking into his apartment was for the birds.

The bathroom was blessedly clean in a relative way, no more than the usual Portland mold and shower stall grunge. Jorge hurried his way through his morning routine, plus a couple of extra rinse cycles under the showerhead—God, he hated being filthy. There was no getting rid of the ink stains on his hand. They did seem a little faded, at least. Out of the shower he picked his way back across his bedroom to get dressed.

Ordinary clothes, he thought. *Like going to traffic court.* Don't dress to distract. Jeans and a plain green flannel shirt.

Jorge paused for a moment. Those were what he had been wearing on his last hike. When the craziness started.

He put on the clothes anyway. Kitchenette for a bottle of Odwalla organic orange juice and a blueberry Special K bar, then heading out the door with his car keys in his hand to give Venera a piece of his mind.

When he opened the door everything went wrong all over again.

The man outside dressed like a wizard. Or more to the point, dressed like someone who thought he was a wizard. He was a short, fat white guy with piggy eyes that gleamed a dark blue over a salt-and-pepper goatee, with long hair to match. Half-moon glasses in silver frames lined with tiny rhinestones. A floppy hat of chocolate-colored velvet, large enough to lose a housecat in, covered with tiny charms. The wizard's brown velvet coat—complementing the hat—was a cross between a smoking jacket and a Renaissance fair costume, complete with large silver buttons worked in some ornate crest.

"Get out of my way, twinkle toes," said Jorge with his best Venera-growl.

"You need me," the wizard replied.

Jorge placed his hand flat on the wizard's broad chest. He had six inches on the overdecorated little tub. "I ain't got time for your shit."

"The Lansquenet is interested in you."

That stopped Jorge. He pulled his hand back. "Lands-cannay. That's the second time I've heard that word in the last twelve hours."

"Lans-que-net." The wizard spelled it out. Then, "Servants of the land. We, well..." He smiled modestly. "We watch over the earth, or at least our portion of it here in the Northwest."

Jorge had a bedroom full of earth at the moment. "No kidding? You must be friends with Venera and her pet sex witch."

"Ah..." The wizard tapped his lips, serious. "Did you happen to get the other woman's name?"

"No." Which had been kind of weird.

"No matter." His hand stuck out, grabbed Jorge's hand in a sweaty shake. "I am Dagobertus Magnus, Bert to my friends. A key man in the Lansquenet."

"Wizard, right?"

Another modest smile. "In a sense. Technically I'm an Edaphomancer. Someone whose power is, ahem, *rooted*, in the soil."

Jorge wanted to slap the idiot. "You're as crazy as they are."

"No." Bert shook his head emphatically. "Venera fancies herself a power here in the Willamette Valley, a Fluvimancer. A Locan, in the old words she prefers. Power from the rivers. But *she's* crazy. I know what I'm doing."

"Right. Look, I work for the Northwest Watershed Trust. I know from rivers. I also know Venera's a witchy bitch. Right now I got an apartment full of dirt and some real bad dreams to show for it. So you, Mr. Bert the wizard of dirt, are either going to help me get this crap swept back out of my life pronto, or you're heading right back to wing-nut central to commune with the rest of the squirrels and leave me the hell alone."

"It's the girlfriend. That one with no name. She's doing these things to you. The Lansquenet has important purposes. Her spells distract you, make you think the land is reaching out."

"I don't believe in spells," Jorge said, pushing Bert out of the way. He yanked his door shut, giving it the lift-and-twist the swollen frame required in damp weather. "I don't believe in dragons or Bigfoot or beautiful women who vanish with the wind." He stomped down the stairs, the pudgy wizard hurrying after him. At the bottom, Jorge turned to face Bert, who was a step up so that they met eye-to-eye. "I especially don't believe in an apartment full of dirt and leaves. For the love of God, this crap's enough to make me move to Los Angeles!"

"I understand your frustration," Bert said, bobbing after Jorge as he went to look for his car.

It had to be out here somewhere, Jorge thought, ignoring the wizard. He'd driven home last night. He hadn't been drunk.

"The Lansquenet can set these things to right. Venera is misguided. That other woman, a sex magician of the worst sort. Very much against all our interests. They always are. Subordinate to the almighty orgasm. Don't integrate with the ebb and flow of—"

"Shut up." Jorge stood at the corner of Milwaukie and Franklin. "Where the hell is my car?"

"Oh," said Bert in a small voice. Almost a squeak.

The mist began to thicken to rain as Jorge thought about that for a moment. "Oh? 'Oh' what?"

"Did you have a little white sedan?"

"I *do* have a BMW 2002tii, yes. It's small. It's white. It's a sedan. I just don't know where it is right now."

"When I got here the city was towing off a car that had been messed up pretty badly." Bert pointed to an open spot in front of the US Bank branch across the street. Shattered glass, paint chips and odd scraps of metal and chrome littered the pavement as if there had been a collision.

Jorge walked over to the scattered junk. He thought he might have parked in front of the ATM last night. Things had been confused. And the paint did match his. Someone had thrown cat litter down over a big stain of oil and gas in the middle of the mess, and the pavement was cracked as if a heavy weight hand landed on it.

"What happened to the car?"

"Crushed by an enormous boulder. They had a big truck from Ross Island cement helping with the rock."

Crushed by a boulder? Jorge turned to stare at Bert. "You're the wizard of dirt. Did you...?"

"Soil, not stone," Bert protested. "Not my power. But can I offer you a ride to work?"

The prospect of mixing Bert with Venera was the best news Jorge had heard all morning. Wherever his car was—and he didn't believe for a minute it had been crushed by a boulder—could wait. He smiled. "Sure thing. I could use the lift."

The QuickSand River appears to pass through the low country at the foot of those high range of mountains in a southerly direction, - The large creeks which fall into the Columbia on the stard side rise in the same range of mountain which we suppose to be Mt. Hood is S. 85E about 47 miles distant from the mouth of quick sand river. This mountain is covered with snow and in the range of mountains which we have passed through and is of a conical form but rugged...
— Journal of William Clark, November 3rd, Sunday, 1805

Bert hummed as he drove. It wasn't far from Jorge's apartment to the Watershed Trust offices at the seedy end of the Hawthorne district, but the traffic was, as always in Portland, shitty. Not Seattle-shitty, thank God, but enough. The dumpy wizard drove like an old man who didn't care when he got there.

Bert had a weird old man car, too, a slightly miniaturized version of an early-1960's tail-finned cruiser. It sported a faded two-tone paint job that had probably once been yellow and white but had averaged towards some union of flyspecked meringue over the years. The inside smelled like, well, dirt.

"Do a lot of gardening?" Jorge asked as he flipped through the owner's manual. *Dear Sir*, it advised him. Did women never buy these cars? The driver in the picture on the cover was a chick in a hat like his grandmother might have worn. He checked the date—1959.

This booklet has been prepared to introduce you to your new Simca Vedette so that you can get to know quickly your new car and enjoy all the good things in motoring it provides.

What language had that been translated from? No normal person would have written it that way. He vaguely recalled that Simcas were French.

"Soil," said Bert in an expansive, hearty tone as if he were launching into a lecture, "is one of the true miracles of life. There are more bacteria in a single handful of healthy soil than there are human beings alive in the

93

world today. Less than one percent of the *species* of soil bacteria have been formally described and classified. And then there are the nematodes. By the land, let me tell you..."

And a lecture it was. Jorge read on, ignoring the man.

Naturally, the first things you will want to know are the locations of the various controls and instruments. We have therefore placed all information covering these and other driving essentials...

They stopped right in front of the head shop over which the Watershed Trust offices were located. The building was a run-down Victorian house with a poorly-executed mural of unicorns and rainbows splashed across the walls. The Simca's brakes squealed and the dirt smell was chased out of the car by a hot oil reek.

"Nice thing about being Skilled," said Bert. "We almost always find parking."

Jorge put the manual back in the glove box and tried to disentangle himself from the Medieval seat belt someone had retrofitted the car with -- the owner's manual certainly hadn't mentioned them. "Skilled. Venera used that word. That's what you New Age types are calling crystal woo-woo this year, I guess."

Bert slammed his door, walked around the car and opened Jorge's door. He reached in to flip the seat belt aside. "We've been calling it that for generations. Regardless of what you believe."

It was the first time Jorge had been moved to take the wizard seriously. "I'm sorry. I just believe so little of this." He climbed out. "Well, none, actually."

"It doesn't matter what you believe," Bert said mildly. "You're the one with the apartment full of dirt and the boulder on your car."

And some really strange dreams, Jorge told himself. It had to be a trick. All of it. *Had* to be.

He led Bert around the side of the head shop to the rickety outside stairs. Up close the crappy paint job was more visible but less obvious. You really had to have some distance to appreciate the artist's ineptness.

As they reached the door, Bert touched Jorge's elbow. "Are you inviting me inside?"

"Inviting?"

"It's important."

Jorge felt a little chill. He still thought the whole business was stupid, but the wizard of dirt clearly took it seriously.

Was there a reason not to invite him in? Venera would...what?

Irritation flooded him, making his face hot. To hell with her. She and eyebrow-girl should have been a lot more forthcoming last night. "Yes. I invite you inside."

Bert smiled. "Thank you."

Jorge pushed the door open. The little bell jingled.

"Hey, skinny butt," said Venera's girlfriend. She was leaning against Jorge's desk in the front part of the office. She gave Jorge a big wink, then licked her finger and touched her hip. "Next time concentrate a little more, *batang lalaki*. You might come to a better end."

She *knew*. She'd been in his dreams. Did that explain the dirt in his bedroom? "How did you—"

Then the little bell on the door rang so hard it popped off its mounting and rolled between Jorge's feet. The wizard of dirt stood beside him. "Well, if it isn't the Fricatrice," said Bert.

Venera's girlfriend's face shut down like sunset on the high desert. She was suddenly hard, looking a lot more dangerous than a woman in a Maggie Simpson t-shirt and Bermuda shorts had any business being. Her eyes stayed on Bert while she jerked her chin at Jorge. "What's the matter with you, skinny butt? You don't got enough trouble, you got to borrow him?"

Jorge felt a cold certainty that he'd made a bad mistake. Words leapt in hot defense to his tongue anyway. "He's no worse than you or Venera. At least he answers my questions."

"We did too, 'til you stopped listening." She shut Jorge out then, as if he'd never been there, focusing on the wizard. "You, dirt boy, get out. This isn't your locus."

"I was invited," Bert said mildly.

"And now you're disinvited." Venera stood in the open door of her office. She was decidedly not smiling.

Jorge's heart sank.

"We're not enemies, Dagobertus Magnus, not yet," Venera continued, "but we're years past when we were last friends. This man is my charge and charter."

"The Lansquenet knows Jorge now. His name is carried on wing and whisper, through root and tunnel, by spring and seep. He has slipped your charge, Fluvimancer."

"I believe the word you are looking for is Locan."

Bert smoothed the sleeves of his velvet coat. "Some of us stay in step with the times. Your opposition to the will of Lansquenet has been troublesome for a while, but I'm afraid you've finally crossed the line, my dear *Locan*."

"Whoever Brought your Five has a lot to answer for, *Éarling*."

"I believe the word you are looking for is Edaphomancer."

They stared at one another until Jorge thought the air would crackle. He didn't understand the underlying argument, but both Venera and Bert were angry about him.

"You know," he said, "I don't give a damn about your Lansquenet. I don't even know what a Locan is. But I can damn well tell when people are talking over my head. I've got a truckload of dirt in my apartment, my car is missing, and I'm two days behind in polling water districts. You guys want to fight, go fight." His voice started pitching higher. "You guys want to help me, help me. Otherwise, *shut the hell up*! Or I'm done with this. My ass will be out of here and to hell with all of you."

"You can't," the Fricatrice said to Jorge. The staring contest between Venera and Bert continued unabated. "The land won't let you."

"Fuck the land!"

Her smile was hard and toothy. "Didn't you try that last night?"

Bert touched Jorge's elbow. "Very well. I'll find you later, Jorge. The Lansquenet will make all this worth your while. We can show you your power."

Then he was gone, the door rattling shut behind him as the fire sprinklers in the office went off and the taps on the sink by the coffee maker burst free atop twin fountains of water.

Venera had chased them out of the Watershed Trust offices with an incoherent screech of rage as soon as the flooding had started. Soggy and irritated, Jorge grabbed a chair in a Salvadoran place down the street. He sat down opposite the Fricatrice. Their table was ridiculously tiny, not much bigger than a waitress' tray, hammered out of old sheet metal.

There was such as thing as taking hip too far.

"*Dos pupusas, por favor,*" the Fricatrice said to the waitress who hovered nearby. The other woman wore a peasant's linen blouse and had a nose fresh off a Mesoamerican idol. "*Y un poco de café. También, un agua del hielo para mi amigo aqui.*"

Jorge watched the waitress head back into the kitchen, then glanced out the window, looking up Hawthorne toward the office. "What was all that?"

"I assume you don't mean the *pupusas.*"

"No."

The Fricatrice sighed. "Well, my friend, the land has awakened to you."

Jorge felt a rush of pressure in his temples, an almost literal boiling over. The logical part of him recognized the fear of strangeness and the bed full of soil. The thought didn't hold back his words. "That's exactly the kind of New Age crap you guys fed me last night, and look where it got me." He slapped the little table, toppling the tiny ceramic cube of sugar packets. "Don't *tell* me that *shit.*"

"What do you want me to say? You saw a dragon, a pretty girl, a hairy man. I didn't do those things to you."

"But you were there, last night."

"You mean late, in your sleep?" She smiled again, softer this time. "In a manner of speaking, yes. You might call it magic, but that's not really what it was."

"Yeah, I know. Skill." He managed to make the word an insult, but she didn't blink. "And the dirt in my bed this morning?"

"You drove me from your dream, invited the land in my place. Like I said, the land awakened to you. It left its calling card."

"And I suppose the land dropped a boulder on my car."

"Unless you think that twit Bert did it."

"He's the wizard of dirt, not rocks."

"Right, as far as it goes. And damned good the Trust offices were on the second floor, where Dagobertus Magnus couldn't be properly grounded. You'd best believe Venera did that on purpose."

"Why did the pipes break?"

"Venera was trying to drive him away. She really is a Locan, a water wizard. Bert pulled a sucker move when he just stepped away from her pressure. She must have been angry, to lose control like that."

"At him or at me?"

"You guess."

His ice water and coffee arrived while Jorge was thinking that over. The Fricatrice made a nasty sludge of hers with six or eight sugar packets and most of the little clay pot of cream. He kept his black, but chose to let it cool, enjoying the sharp scent of the roasted beans.

"It all comes back to what I saw in the woods," he said.

"The land is...the land. It's not a thinking being, not like you or me, but it has a mind. Purposes. A sense of self-preservation. The land is holistic. Venera concerns herself with the waters. Dagobert is one with the soil. You may be something else. Someone who can see the land's intent."

"As a dragon in the trees?"

She sipped at her sludge. "Why would the land send a stone to your car? Think in simple terms."

"To keep me from driving away, I guess. That's the most basic answer."

"Right. It wants you around for something."

He decided to keep pretending this was real. "The pretty girl the other day. The one I fell in love with in a moment. Like it wanted to bind me here."

"Good. Why?"

He remembered the map tattooed on the Sasquatch's back. "I saw Mt. Hood as a glaring eye. Orange, like fire."

Another sip. "Something is coming."

"I don't know what, though."

"I don't know, either. But the land sent the dragon to you for a reason."

"Did Venera know this...land thing about me?" He couldn't figure out how he felt about that. It bothered him to think that his feelings for her might have been manipulated by that Skill crap, too. "Is that why she hired me, kept me around?"

The Fricatrice just smiled over her coffee sludge.

In 1862, the Oregon Steam Navigation acquired both of the portage tramways (north and south sides of the Columbia River) in the present-day Cascade Locks area. The Oregon Pony remained in operation on the Oregon side of the river while OSN reconstructed and improved the portage railroad on the north side of the river. The portage railroad on the north side of the river was incorporated as the Cascades Railroad Company in Washington Territory as a subsidiary of Oregon Steam Navigation. It was six miles long, built to a track gauge of five feet, and was built from the start to standards that would allow for operation with steam locomotives.

— A History of the Oregon Steam Navigation Company,
by Glenn Laubaugh of the National Railway Historical Society

Later they went looking for Jorge's car. The Fricatrice — he still didn't know her name, but figured that her anonymity was one of those Skill things — didn't have a car either, but she had a bus pass and she wasn't afraid to use it.

"Busses are a great place for Skilling," she told him as the number 14 rumbled fitfully toward downtown and the Portland Police Bureau. "Every kind of energy you could want, all in one place. Sexual desperation, drug addiction, ghosts — you name it."

"Ghosts." As if. On the other hand, there was all that dirt in his bed. Were ghosts any more unlikely? He squirmed in the plastic seat. "On the bus. What would a ghost want on a bus?"

"A bus is a place, skinny butt." She glanced at him with that leering smile. "A locus. Locii can be important in Skill. And to ghosts. Those poor bastards need places. Most places don't move around. Busses do. Ergo, ghosts on the bus."

Jorge studied the bus's interior. Signs overhead advised him not to eat, to keep his music private, where to convert his life experience to college credits. Two Mexican guys at back chatted quietly about women and work. A wall-eyed black kid bobbed his head to some private music without the apparent benefit of headphones. A pair of women dressed for the office — coming back from an early lunch, maybe at this hour? — sat not quite touching, ignoring each other and everyone else on the bus.

"I don't know, man. It's just a way to get around."

"And you know what else? Skill is just a way to get by. Some people speak Italian, some people juggle, some people got Skill."

"Juggling doesn't attract so many weirdoes."

All he learned at the Police Bureau was that his car had been impounded as inoperable, and he owed them $345. Irritated but unsurprised, Jorge thanked the public information officer and left without paying. He and the Fricatrice wound up walking down by the Willamette in Tom McCall Waterfront Park. The park was a pleasant stretch of greensward a couple of blocks wide separating the Old Town district of Portland from the river proper. It was a fine example of no-profit urban planning from that long lost era when people thought their tax dollars ought to be spent on the public good instead of refunded. Later infusions of krusties, homeless and the just plain strange hadn't succeeded in robbing the park of its charm.

Jorge studied the Willamette with a professional eye. The river's color shifted between olive green and muddy brown depending on the light. Topsoil runoff upstream, agricultural waste, dumping from the shipping in port. And Portland had a serious problem with sewage overflow mixing with storm water runoff. The city was fixing it. Slowly.

It made Jorge sad to see what so many people had done to the water.

"Can't eat the fish," he said.

"Rivers are bound, land man." The Fricatrice took his hand, held it as they walked.

Friend, he wondered, or guard. Guardian, maybe. Still, the warmth of her grip was comforting. It made him think of Venera. Like the three of them were a chain.

She continued her thought. "White men brought the first rails in all those years ago, tied the Columbia and the Willamette both down with ribbons of steel. Then the dams later on. Nothing but prisons for the river's spirit. Steamboats were more honest than locks and railways. At least they worked with the river, not against it."

He thought about the map on the Sasquatch's back, looked around the grassy park. "There's no steel right here."

"Redevelopment is all. Rail used to run on this side too. Still does, north and south of this break. The river, it has rail chains. Animals can't get to the water, rising mist has to cross cold iron."

"Look, maybe I can believe this land thing and maybe I can't. But why are railroads bad? People live on the land, we need railroads to live. Stuff has to get to stores, whatever. Otherwise we'd all still be sleeping with our cows in little huts. Railroads have got to be better than highways."

It was a discussion that ran endlessly at the Watershed Trust, and every other environmentalist movement that didn't fall in the absolutist camp of Earth First. Use versus conservation. People could be as passionate about this as about capital punishment or abortion.

She squeezed his hand. "You'd fit right in at a Lansquenet gathering, skinny butt. They've been arguing this point for well over a century."

"Jorge. My name is Jorge. Not 'skinny butt.'"

"Jorge." Another squeeze. His groin got that warm tickle. "All you had to do was ask. Jorge the land man. You could have been Brought to Skill, you know. That's part of what the land can see in you. You ever see Colors? Like, auras on things?"

"Auras." He snorted. "No. And I don't need no Skill Bringing. I like being me."

He wondered if that was true. Early thirties, single, lots of time in the Oregon wilderness, socially progressive job, dated—and sometimes fucked—socially progressive woman. If they weren't strict vegan, and he met all the other criteria which were important that week. It had been the right shampoo in his bathroom for one chick. No animal testing here, dude. But where was it all going? He had a good time, mostly

Until the last few days.

"The land doesn't care what you like," she said. "It doesn't think of you as an individual. The land is everywhere, everything. That's why the Lansquenet is in a twist about you. They're the servants of the land. They've been at it for generations. Doing good sometimes, mostly just debating themselves to death. And here you come along, some random normal as the focus of everything they've worked for."

"Are the Lansquenet all Skilled?"

"Just about. Along with a few very dedicated normals. But the Lansquenet are dangerous to the rest of us. They don't play by the Skilled rules."

"Which are...?"

Another squeeze. He had a quick flash of his sweaty sex dream of the night before. She was taking him there again, this time in the flesh. It would be like fucking Venera at one remove. How weird that was, he didn't know.

"Only one way to learn those rules, Jorge the land man."

That was when he heard the dragon scream.

Jorge dropped the Fricatrice's hand, spun with his arms out, already wondering what he thought he was doing. She shouted something he couldn't make out as two burly kids on skateboards ran him down—no, grabbed him.

He kicked, trying to fight the leather-clad krusties, but his thin strength was no match for their muscles. Not to mention the lassitude which settled over him almost immediately.

The Fricatrice ran after him only to be assaulted by a cloud of pigeons. Jorge tried to screech blue murder, but the same inertia which had overcome his abortive struggle against his captors seemed to have settled on his tongue.

No one was watching anyway except the ragged-winged dragon soaring high over the Burnside Bridge as the krusties bundled Jorge into the back of a faded yellow Simca Vedette.

They tied that big old river
They dammed up that big old water
Mississippi of the West
They put you to the test
And made you into something you're not

There's farmers up upon them highlands
There's loggers on wooded mountainsides
Waiting for that power
Waiting by the hour
Them poor folks been waiting all their lives

I hear the engines moaning
I see them barge boats straining
Columbia's she's in hock
Chained to dock and lock
Only her old spirit is complaining
　　　　　— "Columbia River Blues," Abednego "Bargepole" Adams, 1940

Jorge lay slumped in the back of Bert's Simca as the car jerked through stop and go traffic, made some turns, rumbled across one of Portland's drawbridge decks, then eventually settled into the smooth rhythm of highway driving. Maybe Interstate 84, but face down and essentially paralyzed, he couldn't lift himself to look out the windows and check. His body still wouldn't respond. It was as if he had been shot with one of those Mutual of Omaha Wild Kingdom tranquilizer guns.

"Relax." It was Bert the wizard of dirt up front, of course. "As if you weren't already. Heh heh. I apologize for the inconvenience, but the Lansquenet requires your presence. That dreadful woman was drawing you further into her libidinous spell. Trust me, this is for your own good."

Trust, thought Jorge, would be easier to come by if he hadn't been dumped in the back of a car.

"Some of us think you are Skilled, and playing dumb. For myself, I believe that you are a terribly lucky normal, perhaps a wild Skill. Or some odd project of Venera the Fluvimancer and her dreadful Fricatrice. In any of those cases, you are a significant challenge to many in the Lansquenet. I consider myself more open-minded, but that of course comes with being so, ahem, earthy."

Bert chuckled at his own wit and rambled on about nematodes for a while. Jorge studied the carpet fibers and tried to decide if the dragon he'd seen soaring overhead had really been there. And why it had looked so ragged.

That part worried him.

That fact that he was worried told Jorge he believed in the land.

Maybe he always had and never knew it before.

Lack of muscle control apparently did nothing to keep Jorge from feeling all the aches and pains of his cramping body. Bert nattered on for what felt like hours until the Simca exited the highway and dipped long and slow to the right. They went through a series of tight, careful turns. Old man driving in an old man car. Jorge prayed to God the trip was almost over. Even if he was going to be manhandled by more krusties, it had to be an improvement over the floor of the Simca.

Plus he had to pee real bad.

Bert stopped for a murmured conversation—security? Why couldn't the guard see him?—then on again, winding back and forth some more, across the buzzing metal of a bridge deck, the clack of rails.

The car finally ground to a halt with a familiar squeal-and-reek. The back doors opened immediately and people pushed and pulled at Jorge to drag him out of the back seat. They were having such a hard time moving him that he figured the Lansquenet were not kidnapping pros.

"Just unbind him, then," said a testy voice, an older woman. Much older.

After that he was out of the car and up with someone's hands cradling his armpits to face a small crowd. It was like a New Age retreat. They were all dressed as outré as Bert the dirt wizard. Flowing skirts in earthy colors, beaded vests, veils, all manner of amethysts and moonstones and silver charms.

With that thought Jorge found his tongue. "The Lansquenet, I presume?" He didn't bother to hold the nasty out of his voice.

"Keep a civil tongue in your head, young man!" That was the testy old woman again, a tiny thing with a pair of metal crutches. She was wrapped in scarlet silk and wearing an improbably feathered hat.

"Make your God damned invitations more civil next time," Jorge growled.

"Enough," said Bert. "We should repair to our meeting." He grabbed Jorge's elbow, whispering, "Come on, or things might become unpleasant."

Jorge looked around as they walked across an open parking lot. The rain had cleared during his involuntary car ride and afternoon sunlight flooded the scene. There was a scattered assortment of vehicles, most of them as self-consciously odd as Bert's Simca. The lot was on a bluff, with cottonwood trees and sugar elms nearby, and a 1970's-modern building ahead with some landscaping in front of it. There was water on both sides of the lot, and a hell of a lot of industrial concrete.

They were somewhere on the Columbia. After a moment he recognized the layout of powerhouses, shipping lock and islands—it was Bonneville Dam, the lowest dam on the river and a flagship project of the WPA years. That meant this had to be the Bradford Island Visitors' Center.

Then the whole crowd clattered through the lobby of a little interpretive museum with cheery waves to the docent and small bills casually slipped into the donation box. They banged through a blue fire door into a concrete stairwell decorated with paintings of leaping salmon and headed downward accompanied by the swish of silk and the ringing of dozens of tiny bells.

The last thing he saw as Bert pushed him into the stairwell was a view of the river to the west, the ragged dragon circling over the mist-wreathed bluffs on the south side like an errant shadow.

Jorge realized that whatever the Lansquenet had in mind for him, only he could do something about it. The Fricatrice was far behind in Portland, and Venera...well, he wasn't sure about Venera, except for her mounting anger. And he was under no illusions regarding the Lansquenet—they might look like a gaggle of half-stoned old hippies, but these people could control his muscles and bend his mind at a whim.

And they were mad at him. He'd screwed up whatever game they were playing with the land and their self-appointed stewardship over it.

He wondered if his sightings of the dragon had been a good thing or a bad thing. How the hell did this Skill thing work? Did he just somehow start thinking, *here, dragon, dragon, dragon*, and hope for rescue?

If it was that simple, everyone would be doing it.

After the kindness of a brief pit stop in a restroom at the bottom of the stairs, Bert marched Jorge into a largish room finished out in slightly dated museum-kitsch. Sunlit doors exited at both ends of the room. Carpeted floors, large glass cases with models of fish in them, blue directional signage painted over the concrete walls, posters with fish identification information, and a set of varnished backless benches arranged before a pair of windows behind which there was...water.

And fish.

They were in the fish counting room. And there were lots of fish. Squirming, swimming, thrashing against a turbulent current the color of old tea. Salmon, shad, lampreys, all in a boiling silver mass against the windows.

Jorge stared. In September the salmon run was trailing off. It was way late for shad. Lamprey were rare at any time.

The land was reaching out to him. He could feel a slow wave of cold-blooded intent through the windows. Something between panic and anger.

Then the Lansquenet swirled around him. Fingers brushed against his cheek, touched his hair, plucked at his clothes. It was like being mobbed by the Gray Panthers.

That was when Jorge realized what was odd about the Lansquenet. They were all old. Bert was the youngest, given Jorge's not very precise impression of the others, and even Bert had to be in his fifties. Venera was exactly the same age as Jorge—thirty-three—and he'd bet the Fricatrice was still in her twenties.

That had to mean something. Where did the younger Skilled go to serve the land? People of his generation and the kids coming up after cared passionately about the environment. The Skilled among them would be naturals for the Lansquenet.

On the other hand, there was certainly a near-violent opposition between Venera and Bert.

Bert tugged Jorge around the perimeter of the room to stand in front of a smaller door which stood ajar very close to one of the fish windows. Inside was a video set up and a metal-faced board of switches sort of like an old-fashioned mechanical calculator, all facing another fish window.

The fish counter's station. And no doubt the Lansquenet had sent the fish counter out for coffee with a side of amnesia. Or maybe arsenic.

Jorge grinned in spite of himself.

The old woman in scarlet stood in front of the fish windows with her hands pressed together like a Buddhist at prayer, crutches propped against her elbows. She closed her eyes, began to hum, and quickly the chatter of Lansquenet died down. Someone rang a bell—silver, no doubt—and the old woman's humming reached a crescendo.

"Honor to the earth that is mother to us all," she intoned.

"Honor to the earth," echoed the Lansquenet.

Jorge took advantage of their moment of ritual to count heads.

"Honor to the air that lends us life with every breath."

"Honor to the air."

Twelve, fourteen...

"Honor to the water that fills our veins and slakes our thirst."

"Honor to the water."

Twenty-seven, twenty-eight. Plus the old woman in red, Bert, and himself.

"Honor to the fire that is in our bellies and in our souls."

"Honor to the fire."

She opened her eyes and stared at Jorge. He was surprised to see that her irises were almost as orange as the eye on the Sasquatch's back in his dreams.

Dreams.

Was that his way out?

"This gathering of the Lansquenet is now in session. I am Edith, a Pyretic of the witch line of Joanna and as senior-most I name myself speaker of the gathering."

"Honor to you, Edith," said the Lansquenet, their response more ragged than the tight timing and cadence of the opening ritual.

This was nothing like the aggressively casual way Venera and the Fricatrice seemed to approach their magic.

No, he thought. *Skill*. Call it what it was for them.

Jorge wondered if he did have Skill. Was Skill really like Italian? Or juggling? The Fricatrice had suggested it was just another talent, after all.

"Our Great Unbinding is near its end," Edith said. Jorge was startled at the venom in her voice. "A project we have worked toward for two generations. And those...children...in the city claim to have found a new favorite of the land. As if any Landesmann could arise now in the Northwest from outside our ranks. The Lansquenet is all."

"The Lansquenet is all," repeated the audience.

That echo was starting to creep him out pretty badly. At least he was beginning to understand the reluctance of the younger Skilled to join the Lansquenet. He was torn between a sense of their silliness and fear of their seriousness.

"You!" Edith pointed at Jorge. "Why do you set yourself in opposition to us?"

"Me? Your boy Bert sought me out. I've got nothing to do with opposing the Lansquenet."

"You have set yourself up as a false Landesmann."

"I don't even know what the hell a Landesmann *is*."

"You claim to have called the land to you. You claim to have seen it in dreams. You claim the land has followed you, spoken to you, become one with you."

His night-dream of the Fricatrice and the Sasquatch had definitely been a "becoming one with" kind of experience, but Jorge wasn't about to discuss that with Edith. "I don't claim anything here. All I know is I've been kidnapped and brought against my will."

"Easy, Jorge," said Bert, still standing beside him. "Those are strong words. We're you're friends. Edith's just doing *pro forma* business."

"*Pro forma* my left foot, Dagobert," said Edith. "This little punk isn't going to interfere with the Great Unbinding. Not on my watch."

"And what is the Great Unbinding?" asked Jorge. Behind him the fish counting windows rattled slightly. He felt a chill, like he had that day in the woods, and his mouth tasted of old leaves and cold stone.

This was close to the heart of whatever crisis had sent the land to him in the first place, he realized.

"Nothing that concerns you any further, young man."

Could these nuts make Mt. Hood erupt? That would explain the orange eye in the Sasquatch's back, and his warning about the dancing stones. But he couldn't even begin to imagine why they would do such a thing. Mt. St. Helens was a sufficiently recent memory here in the Pacific Northwest to keep anyone from having fond illusions about the restorative powers of volcanic eruptions.

The river. That was why they were here, in the fish counting room. "You want to free the waters," he whispered. The dancing stones would be the dam collapsing.

Bert jabbed Jorge in the ribs with his fingers. "Shut up, boy. Don't ask for trouble."

"So you do have a head on those pretty shoulders," Edith said. "Water is the blood of the land. That blood is bound by steel and concrete, which we must overcome. You raise yourself as a false Landesmann in opposition to our work, claiming power over earth and air, water and fire."

"You're not listening to me!" Jorge shouted. "I'm not opposing anybody in anything." Now he *was* lying. The thought of these nuts blowing the Bonneville Dam horrified him. But he couldn't fix that right now. Not yet. He had to get out of there, alive and with his memories intact. "I can't help it if something came to me. I don't know what it was. I don't want to know."

Don't deny the land, whispered a voice in his head. The dragon? The Fricatrice?

He heeded it. "Maybe it was the land," he continued. "I've seen miracles of water and earth this very day. But this has nothing to do with the Lansquenet. If it is the land, the land chose me."

"Lies." Edith literally waved Jorge off. She was flushing to match her fiery silk wrap. "Self-serving piffle. The Lansquenet are the servants of the land. If it sought a true Landesmann, it would have reached among our worthy Edaphomancers and Fluvimancers and Aeolians and Pyretics."

The members of the Lansquenet murmured as Bert's grip on his arm tightened to the point of pain. Hard gazes turned on Jorge. He saw his death in pursed lavender lips, long glossy fingernails, swept back graying hair, the pulled-tight crows feet of angry eyes. It was like being cursed by every grandparent he'd ever met.

And so this comes down to jealousy, he realized.

Edith placed her palms together again. "I call upon the will of the Lansquenet in this matter."

How was he going to get out of this? Jorge had no doubt of these peoples' menace towards him. Bert wouldn't meet his eye now. The crowd of Skilled were talking amongst themselves in the indistinct muttering voice of a mob, angry cadences rising and falling.

Landesmann. Power over earth and air, water and fire. Which meant...dirt in his bed and rocks on his car.

But he'd been distracted, almost in a dream state when he saw the dragon. The same for the girl. And asleep and truly dreaming when the Sasquatch came and the dirt happened.

The soil in his bed proved the Skill-magic was real.

The voices of the Lansquenet were trailing off. Agreement was being reached. To his right, the fish squirmed against their windows, their presence a cold pressure against his mind.

I have to dream, Jorge thought. The land comes when it wants to, as dragon, woman or Sasquatch; but I can only call it to me in my dreams.

How the hell was he going to dream on demand?

He could pick a fight, right here, but they might just as well kill him as knock him unconscious. He couldn't make a break through the room and out the doors—and how the hell were there doors down this many flights of stairs?

The bell rang again. Edith looked far too satisfied with herself for Jorge's peace of mind.

"I'll speak for you," said Bert quietly.

Right, Jorge thought. *Dreams. Now.* He urgently imagined the ragged dragon swooping down from the cliffs along the south bank, skimming from mist to sunshine like a falling leaf to rescue him.

The fish swirled against the glass like fingers tapping on a windowpane.

Fish. Fish don't dream, but I do.

Just as Edith began to pronounce judgment, Jorge threw his elbow hard into Bert's ribs, following up with a punch that slid past the dirt wizard's jaw but clobbered him in the ear. Then Jorge stepped backward into the fish counter's station and slammed the door.

It had a deadbolt lock, which he threw. He dragged the desk with the video equipment in front of the door.

There was a tall, narrow window next to the door, partially obscured by a fish poster. He could see Edith hammering on the glass with one metal crutch, so he grabbed a couple of other posters that were hanging in the tiny office and crammed them into the metal-framed space of the window.

"Screw you, fire-woman!" Jorge shouted.

Then he turned to face the fish.

They mobbed this window now, thicker than ever, a solid wall of scales, fins and colors. What he had thought at first glance to be silver was a mass of glinting hues, from red-bodied sockeye salmon to the rainbow sheen of the steelhead.

Jorge tugged the counter's chair right up to the glass and sat down, leaning his head against the window. The cold pressure was the hand of the river on his forehead, like a mother checking a fevered child. Fish flickered in front of him.

"Send me some dreams, guys," Jorge whispered as the pounding began.

He pushed his thoughts outward toward the fish, following that pressure they had been placing on him. It was like counting sheep. One by one, his thoughts left, each carried away by a single fleeing fish, until he slipped into unconsciousness even as the door behind him hummed and smoked with the anger of the wizards of the Lansquenet.

Scars left by the powerful current mark the high narrow walls of the [Columbia River] Gorge to this day. It is evidence that the water got deeper and deeper. As water filled the narrow channel, the depth reached more than a thousand feet. The flow accelerated to 90 miles an hour, gathering an increasing payload of debris. The Gorge contained most of the raging

water — an overwhelming torrent aimed directly at what is now Portland.
— David Hulse of the University of Oregon in
Ice Age Flood: Catastrophic Transformation of the West,
Oregon Public Broadcasting

The ragged dragon circled over the three islands in the Columbia, stiff with the scent of damp firs and forest mold. Watching over its shoulder, Jorge could see the narrow lines of concrete stretching from bank to island to island to bank like the garden paths of a drunken industrial giant. Water upstream glittered placid behind the great walls, while downstream it boiled from the spillways and powerhouses. The islands and dams themselves were a complex arrangement of cranes and railroad tracks and vast metal gates, power lines strung between them on towers painted orange and white, the whole thing tinker toys for the giant's child.

He shifted his attention to the dragon itself. Its wings were a vast, mottled patchwork of autumn leaves and narrow veins of wood, an airplane built by woodland spirits. The body was little more substantial, a prickly collection of twigs and pine needles like a giant thatch ant nest.

In a way, it was a giant maple leaf in flight. Jorge clung to the dragon's wooden spine with hairy hands that seemed familiar, though they were not his own in waking life.

Down, he told the dragon.

His gaze slid toward the parking lot of the visitors' center out on Bradford Island in the middle of the river. A familiar faded yellow car sat near the front doors, surrounded by faux-gypsy redwood camper shells and pre-Jerry Garcia VW bus-pickup hybrids.

There.

As the dragon circled closer, Jorge tried to figure out where the fish windows were. He quickly realized that the building was four or five stories tall, the front which faced the parking lot actually being the top of the building. From the other side, the structure descended with the slope of the bluff that was the center of Bradford Island until it footed in a little maze of walkways, landscaping, and the narrow, churning channel of a fish ladder.

The other side of the building.

The dragon swooped lower, creaking like a forest in the wind. A walkway bridged a lower one that seemed to lead to the bottom level of the visitors' center. The dragon spilled air from its wings to come to a shuddering landing on the bridge. It extended its neck downward and peered into the double glass doors where the lower walkway met the building.

A pale face pressed against the doors from the inside for a moment, then vanished with a shriek.

Jorge smiled with satisfaction, and jumped from the dragon to shamble onward in rescue of himself. On the ground, he realized how huge he was. The map tattooed on his back itched, up by his shoulder the hardest.

He burst through the doors without opening them first, howling and venting his musk in the spray of glass splinters.

Jorge's head snapped back as he jolted awake. For a moment he felt witless. The fish were gone, leaving only tea-colored water behind. The counting station reeked of electrical smoke and incense.

Outside, people were shouting.

There was no other way out except through that room.

He somehow felt overly short and thin as he pushed the table back from the door, as if he'd returned to childhood. The door handle was too hot to touch, so he grabbed one of the fish posters from the narrow window and wrapped his hand in it.

Out in the fish counting room there was chaos. The varnished benches were overturned as people surged back and forth. The Sasquatch from Clark's bar—and in fairness, from his dream—roared an incoherent challenge as it shambled through the room. Most of the Lansquenet were either panicked or awestruck. A swirl of red caught his eye as Edith fled by the south doors all the way across the room, followed by Bert, his brown velvet coat flapping.

And if Bigfoot was in here, the dragon must be outside the north doors.

Jorge pushed through the crowd as hard as he would have moshed at the Aladdin. These old dudes might have made the scene at Woodstock, but they'd never done smashmouth punk. And no one had the concentration for Skill-magic at this moment.

As he made his way toward the dragon, Jorge could have sworn the Sasquatch winked at him. Then he was out the shattered doors in sunlight, staring into a vast pale eye the texture and color of a queen ant's abdomen.

This is it, he thought. This is where the dreams and the magic and the frou-frou New Age Skill bullshit become real.

Not the dirt in his bed.

Not the boulder on his car.

This dragon of leaf and wood and insect parts, that he could mount and fly to chase down Edith and Bert before they did something truly regrettable to Bonneville Dam.

Do you believe? he asked himself.

He patted the dragon's mossy muzzle just below the eye. It reeked of the land, forests and fields and cold, hard mountain rock—much ranker than the gentle pine scent of his dream. "Did you come for me, girl?" It was a she, he realized. Was all the land female?

Not the Sasquatch, certainly.

The dragon's head dipped a little further, nearly pulling her off balance from her perch on the walkway above. Jorge grabbed the neck, which despite seeming so fragile took his weight easily, then hoisted himself up to sit above her shoulders, just before the roots of her wings.

She leapt upward, flapping hard to make air, spiraling away from the visitors' center and the roadways surrounding it. Jorge clung to her rough-textured neck in a spot where all her materials seemed to come together in one leathery skin and watched for the flash of red that was Edith's silk.

He'd never spot Bert the dirt wizard from up here.

As they rose higher, he glanced for the parking lot. The yellow Simca was still there. Then he saw the color he was looking for. Edith and Bert were by the north side of the first powerhouse, the dam section linking Bradford Island with Robins Island where the navigation lock was.

"There they are!" Jorge shouted.

The dragon wheeled and dove. Swooping toward the powerhouse, his gut finally felt the reality of being in the air, essentially unrestrained. He felt a moment of eye-watering panic tinged with vertigo before that was overtaken in turn by the realization that the dragon was diving right into the north wall of the powerhouse.

There were three tall metal doors there, each large enough to pass turbine sections or generator housings. Jorge prayed the dragon was going for one of those instead of the solid concrete of wall.

And go for them it did, Jorge screaming his lungs out as the dragon exploded against the central door in a cloud of dust, dirt, sticks and leaves. The door ripped open with a boom like a giant's footfall as Jorge was thrown inward, riding a wave of forest debris to tumble flat on a concrete floor surrounded by interpretive museum signage.

The dust settled as klaxons began to wail. Venera stood up from behind a picture of the dam being built. "What the hell took you so long, Jorge?" She was smiling.

His heart jumped in his chest. "Oh, God." He wanted to kiss her, but there wasn't time. "Edith," he gasped. "Bert." The roiling dirt made him cough.

She cocked her head, nodding down to the powerhouse floor.

Jorge pulled himself to his feet and looked.

They were on an observation balcony at one end of a room that had to be a thousand feet long, and at least ten stories high. Generator housings receded into the distance like a series of mechanical wedding cakes, while a partially-assembled turbine awaited more blades on the floor beneath them. The hub of the turbine was about the size of his lamented car.

The walls and floors were tiled in ocher-and-brown geometric patterns, ornamentation from an age when people built even industrial facilities to please the eye. The safety orange of the overhead gantry cranes was a jarring contrast, as was the red Corps of Engineers logo painted on the nearest generator housing.

"Damn it," he said, recovering his breath. "They must be out on the generator floor already. Now what?"

Venera's smile grew toothy. "This is a dam powerhouse, Jorge. We're standing *on top* of the Columbia River. Fire-woman and earth-boy down there are about to learn not to fuck with a Locan over running water."

In that moment, he knew his love for her was real, not just a crush or a Skill charm. And he thought he could see a spark in her eyes, too. Grinning he asked, "Can I watch?"

"Count on it, Landesmann."

When she leapt over the rail, he followed her without even looking first.

They scurried around the downstream curve of the second generator housing. Equipment carts stood nearby, and their sightlines were obscured by cabling and pillars. Everything smelled of machine oil and the tight, crispy tingle of lots and lots of electricity. Doors boomed open to the distant shouts of security guards. Jorge reflected that you could hide a boatload of old hippies in a place this big and complex.

Venera placed a hand flat on the generator housing. The great slab of metal hummed slightly. Jorge could feel a vibration through the floor. "How are you going to—"

"Shh." She waved him to silence and bowed her head for a moment. Then, "The water tells me. It doesn't like Pyretics. Natural opposition."

"Is that why she wants to blow the dam?"

"Water is power, Jorge." Her fingers brushed his, sending a spark of static between them. "Now come on."

They sidled on around the housing, keeping as close as the cabling and support struts would allow. Venera pointed at the next housing.

Judging by the echoes the shouting security guards seemed to be getting closer.

Jorge scurried after Venera as she dodged across the open space between the generator housings. She did not pause this time, but kept racing around the curve toward the upstream side, fingers trailing against the metal.

The hum from this turbine sounded different to Jorge, as if it were spinning harder. Was she calling the water? He tried to feel the force of the land in his mind, the water flowing as its blood, but outside of his dreams, Jorge had little control.

Love or no love, he would have felt better if the Fricatrice had been around for this little showdown. Strength in numbers.

Venera stopped suddenly. "Get your lousy asses out here, *now*," she shouted. "No more warnings."

A brilliant snake of flame came arcing around the generator housing. Venera ducked it without losing her contact with the housing, while Jorge simply hit the floor. It splashed against the posts behind him supporting the service catwalk that reached the tops of the generator housings. Sparks spit where it hit—a power connection cut?

"Hey, Landesmann." Venera's voice was distant, as if she concentrated hard.

The turbine was definitely whining hard now, the concrete floor thrumming.

"What?"

"Keep them off me another minute or so. And if I can't get the genie back in the bottle, you'll have to ask the land to do it."

"I don't know —"

Then a shambling man-mound of sticks and leaves and soil came around the curve of the housing.

A sending from Bert. Made from the remains of Jorge's ragged dragon. There wasn't anyplace else to get that much organic matter from down in here.

It was like pissing in a church. "God damned dirt wizard!" Jorge shouted.

He sprinted past Venera and charged into the man-mound shoulder first. It was like running into a tree. Jorge bounced off, his arm in agony.

The man-mound reached for him with a large, indistinctly formed fist.

Jorge backed up, banging into some copper piping stacked against one of the pillars supporting the catwalk overhead, perhaps waiting to be installed as a water line. He snagged an eight-foot length and used it to stab at the man-mound.

Keep it at bay, keep it at bay, he though. At bay was fine for a moment or two. How to kill it?

The concrete floor was vibrating now as smoke poured out of the generator housing. Another flame snake shot toward them, but it became diffused by the smoke.

Jorge stabbed again and backed toward the pillar that the first shot had hit.

Bert's sending still followed him.

"You were a dragon," he told it. "Spirit of the land. Look at you now. Bert's made you a mockery of yourself."

The man-mound took another swipe at him.

Jorge could hear sparks spitting overhead. He prayed he wasn't about to bump into a hot line. A quick glance upward showed a slagged junction box.

Aha. Good. Do this just right, he might live long enough to see what Venera was going to do next.

The shambling thing took one step closer and Jorge leaped. He jabbed the back end of the copper pipe into the slagged junction box, feeling a harsh buzz in his palms as he made contact, then spread his hands and fell away, thinking: don't ground yourself, idiot.

The far end of the pipe drooped toward the concrete, spitting sparks, as the man-mound grabbed at it. Power from the junction box grounded through the man-mound. Flares arced all over its body to erupt in bursts of flame as the leaves and wood burned off.

Jorge ran around the other side of the generator housing without waiting to see more. Bert's sending was occupied, and there wasn't any more soil handy to make another—he hoped to God—but he had to distract Edith from shooting more flame snakes, at least until Venera finished her Skilling.

He caught up with Edith and Bert standing over a glowing box. Edith turned to him and shouted, "Aristides will—" just as the arc of the generator housing closest to them burst open with a torrent of Columbia River water, thick with fish.

Somehow, Venera had reversed the turbine and called the water *up*.

It was like a liquid bomb going off. Bert was caught full force by the water jet and smashed backward into the upstream wall of the powerhouse, pulped by the pressure along with dozens of salmon and steelhead. More fish shot out at angles to fall into the glowing box and buffet Edith like giant silver fists. A whole new set of alarms began going off overhead, barely audible over the roar of the river.

Jorge could have cheered. Venera had succeeded. The Lansquenet's spell had been disrupted. But now the genie definitely needed to go back into the bottle, fast. Already the rushing water was tearing at the adjacent sections of the generator housing, and flames shot up out of the top.

Jorge grabbed a wildly thrashing male sockeye, bright red. The fish took a bad bite of his left hand. He held it close to his temple, trying to think in cool, crisp, simple fish-dreams. "Back," he told the water. *Help me, ragged dragon.* "Back." *Help me, Sasquatch.* "Back." The pretty girl drinking his chai smiled, and for a moment the fish was not so cold.

The roar of the water abated then, dying quickly. When Jorge opened his eyes Edith was nowhere in sight. He dropped the sockeye and pushed through the mass of wriggling fish to find Venera curled up on the ground, fingers still on the generator housing. She seemed smaller, wrinkled like a used condom.

Discarded.

I am the Landesmann, he thought. I can bring my love up out of this place.

But there were men with drawn guns and bullhorns on the catwalk overhead, and he had nowhere to go. He scooped up Venera anyway and ran for one of the service doorways leading out to the downstream face of the powerhouse. Bullets whanged off the concrete but missed him as he plunged through the door.

Outside was a roadway with inspection ladders leading upward and downward across the face of the dam. A helicopter clattered overhead, and a whole new family of sirens screamed out here. He just kept running, across the roadway, and leapt into the high space above the lower reaches of the Columbia.

As he fell, still holding tight to Venera, Jorge could see the fish below him parting like hands to admit him to the river's depths.

He came up sputtering for air like every drowning man who'd ever lived. The water was September cold. Power lines marched in the distance upstream, but no one was shooting at him.

Where was Venera?

Jorge splashed around, looking. She wasn't with him. She wasn't nearby. He struck toward shore. Maybe he could spot her from a rock.

"Hey," said the pretty woman in the birchbark canoe. She was dressed differently today, in buckskins to match her boat.

"Venera," he said, grabbing the side for support. Where had this girl come from? She'd done it to him again. "My..." He didn't know what she was. "Thin black woman, a Locan. She's out here somewhere."

"No. She's not. The waters have claimed her." That laugh, the one that pierced his heart all over again. "The river knows its own."

Though it pained his heart, Jorge had to believe her. He was the Landesmann, she was the land.

The girl helped him into the canoe, smiling like she kept all the secrets of the world. A little while later, they landed on a tree-topped gravel bar. She slipped out of her buckskins and offered him some of those secrets, but he refused, miserable for Venera. She smiled and held him to her breast a while and sang river songs until he slept.

When he awoke near sundown with her earthy scents still on him, the land-girl was gone, but her canoe remained. He paddled his way through the evening fog back to Portland, thinking hard without reaching any conclusions.

Jorge didn't know what else to do, so he went back to work the next day. His body ached terribly, and getting dressed was a hassle with all the dirt scattered around his apartment, but the long walk from his neighborhood to the Watershed Trust office seemed to work out the worst of the kinks.

The office was a mess, of course, from the sprinkler incident the day before. The sight of the wreckage made him want to kneel down and weep for Venera, but he could imagine what she'd say about *that*. He had to act as if she was coming back.

So instead he tried to do some actual work. Venera had cleaned up the worst of the flood, and somehow his computer had been spared, though there was already mold growing on the monitor.

Jorge logged into oregonlive.com to see what was what. He hadn't even tried the radio at home. An aborted terrorist attack at Bonneville Dam was all over the headlines. One generator had been badly damaged in the incident, but far worse consequences averted. Apparently a quick-thinking group of senior citizens had spotted some radical environmentalists on the prowl and alerted security. There was mention of a single unidentified casualty. He wondered what had become of Edith.

"That Lansquenet," Jorge told his monitor mold, "always one step ahead."

Later as he was spreading out files to dry, the Fricatrice turned up with two cups of Salvadoran coffee—hers sugar sludge, Jorge's black with a sharp odor that cut right through his fatigue. She was wearing a Trixie t-shirt today, from the old Speed Racer cartoon, and a pair of bicycle pants several sizes too small for her. She gave him a big, sloppy kiss, as if they were old lovers. "You did the right thing, Landesmann."

He asked the one question that was on his heart. "What about Venera?"

"The river knows its own. Maybe she'll be back. She's tough."

"Not tough enough." He brushed the warm sting from his eyes, but he realized the Fricatrice didn't look sad at all. He figured she understood more about all this than he did. Maybe Venera was coming back.

After he regained his composure, Jorge said, "I never could figure it out, you know."

"¿*Que?*"

"Coming down the river last night, I couldn't figure why the Lansquenet wanted to blow the dam. I mean, I understand about the river being chained by steel rails and concrete dams. But they have to live here, too. We're all part of the land, us people with our cities and everything."

"Water is power, *batang lalaki*."

"I know, but why release it?"

She slurped on her sludge, took some time answering. "They got a...vision...for the land. To return it to what it was. Maybe they're not even wrong. I don't know. But as for the river...anybody can feel the power of impounded water. Why do you think there are so many stories of lake monsters? It ain't like there's really dinosaurs swimming around down there with the frog shit. Water holds the memory of what has passed through it, and what it has passed through. Water holds secrets. Water holds death in its murky bonds."

"Like ghosts on the bus. Water is a place. A locus, you said."

She winked. "Exactly. A place that's everywhere and nowhere, always moving. Now maybe you understand what it means to be a Locan like Venera. People who don't have elemental Skills, they think it's fire that's hard, always changing, always calling. Pyretics, they got it easy. Throw a few tantrums, get on with life. Water's the toughest master."

"So why release it?"

"Think of all the power they'd have. There would be a flood, a tiny little Missoula, the symbol of the scouring the Lansquenet would bring to the northwest. Restoring the land. And then the Skill power the flood would give them. Spells to move mountains. Or erase cities." She slurped again. "But they made one big mistake in their thinking—the land is always changing. People are just another part of the change. You think Kennewick Man didn't pee in the river or fish for salmon? Erasing man's hand from the land is like trying to put Mount St. Helens back together."

"Yeah." Something else bothered him, a loose thread. "And Aristides?"

The Fricatrice stared over the plastic lid of her coffee cup for a moment. "Where you hear that name?"

"You and Venera, that first night. Then Edith the Pyretic started to say something about him when Venera blew the generator housing."

"Forget him. He's a different kind of problem. Lots of people think he's their friend, they're all wrong. There isn't a side he hasn't played. You ever hear from him, you run the other way. Then maybe you call me for help."

Jorge smiled. "How would I do that?"

"In your dreams, baby."

After a moment, he realized she wasn't kidding. "I see."

"No. You don't. But you will. Good-bye, Landesmann." She stood, gave him another sloppy kiss, and walked out.

into the gardens of sweet night

A Chance Meeting by Road

"Penny for your thoughts, stranger."

Elroy glanced around. His mind had wandered as he followed his footsteps down the ancient metal highway. No one was in sight.

He felt a tug on the leg of his trousers.

"Down here, stranger. Fancy a Justiciary penny?" The voice was high, almost squeaky.

Elroy looked down. A tan pug dog with a black face and ears trotted on its foot paws next to him, one thumbed paw loosely caught in the muslin of his trousers at the level of his right knee. The pug wore a green flowered waistcoat.

At two meters in height, Elroy towered far over the Animal. "A Justy penny? Truly?"

"Spend 'em anywhere," said the pug with pride. The dog's brown eyes darted back and forth, while a long tongue licked its nose. Its curly little tail wagged quickly.

Considering the unmodified muzzle, Elroy thought the pug had a remarkably clear voice. It offered him the promised penny in its right thumbed paw. Without breaking his stride, Elroy leaned down and grasped the coin. He slipped it into his belt pouch. Justies spent anywhere, not like the various city scrips backed only by faithless reputations and threat of local violence.

Elroy was returning from a year-long spirit quest among the Little Brothers of High Impact in the Glass Mountains of Oklahoma. He was headed home to his family's little treetop cabin in the rain forest around

Pilot Knob. Elroy wanted to climb lianas, gather bananas in the clearings, and hunt tamarin monkeys in the high forest canopy. He wanted to court a familiar girl, wed the old-fashioned way, and raise a family up in the trees as Texans always had. Which required funds, something he had in small supply after a year in a monastery. And he was still five hundred kilometers from home, a long lonely walk down the decrepit highway.

The pug tugged again at his trousers. "Well?"

"Animals." Elroy shot a sidelong glance at the pug. "I am thinking about Animals."

The pug sidestepped away, disappointment flashed in his canine eyes. His tail drooped. "I did not pay for an insult, friend."

"You neither bought my friendship with a Justiciary penny, stranger," snapped Elroy. "But I won't insult you. I said Animals, not beasts."

"Your thoughts, then?" The pug growled and narrowed its eyes.

Elroy could see the pug's hackles rise above the collar of its waistcoat. He sighed, regretful for having mishandled the situation so quickly. "What is servant to a mounted man, peer to a footed man, and master to a legless man?"

The pug's hackles dropped back below its flowered collar. "A poor riddle, as you already gave me the answer. Scarcely worthy of my investment."

Elroy slowed, stepping to the roadside next to a weathered sign that read "New Dallas 82 klmtr.s, Fresh Fruit next Left."

"My deepest apologies, gentle pug." Elroy recalled his school days and the whippings he routinely received from Master Stenslaw for inattention the finer points of law and social custom. "I am rarely approached under the terms of the Mutual Contract, and am unversed. I intended no offense."

"None taken, I'm sure," muttered the pug.

"Enough, then." Elroy smiled. "I stop to dine. It's poor fare I have, but I offer it freely."

The pug laughed, a strangled bark. Its tail flickered again. "I like generosity in the young. They are usually too callow to comprehend the value of a gift freely given. Let us instead repair to the fruit vendor ahead. In recognition of your kind offer to share your food, I will stand us a pair of kumquats, or whatever else they might have that suits."

A Dinner of Fruit in the Rainforests of Texas

"Well, you're a couple of likely lads." The old woman at the fruit stand smiled a gap-toothed smile.

"I am hardly a lad, good woman. Do not mistake my size for youth." The pug drummed its claws on the edge of the old woman's table. "We will have two kumquats, and a liter of wine fit for consumption."

"No kumquats today. Guavas three for a New Dallas dollar, I'm out of wine but you can have sweet plum jack two NewDees a liter," she recited in a bored voice.

"Two Justies for the guavas and the plum jack," the pug countered.

"Three."

They bargained in a desultory manner, settling on two Justiciary pennies and a New Dallas dollar, which the pug handed over from the pocket of its waistcoat.

"Thank you, my good woman." The pug stepped back from the table. "Get our supper, my boy."

Elroy considered arguing that he was not, in any sense, the pug's boy. The smell of the guavas changed his mind, being far more appetizing than the stale bread crusts he had planned to eat. He took the three guavas and the liter of plum jack, served with the loan of a translucent tube bearing white volumetric markings on the side, and followed the pug away from the fruit stand.

They ate in the shadow of the glossy green leaves of a blooming mango tree. Elroy was grateful for the two guavas the pug had generously given him. They passed the plum jack back and forth swig for swig, although Elroy drank considerably more than the pug at each pass. The mango tree sat on a bluff above the highway, giving them an excellent view of several kilometers of the road. In the distance, a land train puffed dark smoke and light steam into the sky, while the heavy scent of the mango blossoms and the drone of insects lulled Elroy toward sleep.

"*Magnifera indica.*" The pug waved at the tree above them. "In Vedic tradition this tree symbolizes abundance and divine sweetness." The pug grasped the tube of plum jack in both thumbed paws and gulped. "Alcohol is dangerous for small dogs," the pug continued, panting. "Slows down their breathing, interferes with the central nervous system."

The conversation worried Elroy. Animals were not beasts, and for the pug to refer to its base canine ancestry so casually violated a widespread taboo. The great projects of the Viridian Republic had long since vanished from history, save for Animals, who now labored in many of the occupations of the world. They carefully fashioned their succeeding generations in their own images, and were equally jealous of their heritage and the secrets of their kind. Elroy held his tongue, choosing silence over potential insult.

"Well," the pug continued after a long pause, "a man who knows when to hold his thoughts." It passed the plum jack to Elroy.

"I am a traveler far from home. It is trouble enough for me to know my own thoughts, let alone mind those of others."

"A worthy attitude. Would that all were as wisely discreet."

Elroy opted for tact. "Discretion is the better part of a man."

The pug studied Elroy closely, licking its nose repeatedly as brown canine eyes scanned his face. "Are you heading home, or setting out?"

It was a question not asked in polite conversation. Elroy recognized the seriousness of the pug's request, gave consideration to its open-handedness with the guavas and the plum jack.

"Returning, sir pug, from a long course of spiritual study and physical pursuits."

"Were you successful?"

Elroy shifted, uncomfortable but trapped by the pug's hospitality and the opening created by his own honest answer. One boy in every generation from his town of Pilot Knob was set out on the road to the Little Brothers. Some returned, some did not. Many who did became village hetmen in their time. Elroy felt no ambition to rule, but he had found balance, strength and a small measure of wisdom among the Little Brothers—qualities he recognized as desirable in a future leader. "Yes, I succeeded."

"So your duties to faith and family have been fully discharged?"

"Yes. I am free, and bound for home."

"Then I would offer you a post of service with me, for a time." The Animal smoothed the front of its flowered waistcoat, showing more than reflexive nervousness. "My terms are generous, especially if we meet with success in my ventures."

Elroy did not want to take service with the pug, to be distracted from home and finding a bride. On the other hand, starting a family took money, or at least resources. The pug's Justiciary penny had already doubled his savings, and having left the monastery, he was no longer a mendicant.

"What service, what terms, and what is the mark of success?"

The pug licked its nose. "I need a person of discretion and physical skill to assist me as a traveling companion and bodyguard. I offer expenses, board, and a Justiciary penny per day, plus substantial bonuses upon success of my own mission." The pug paused, plucked at its waistcoat as it stared forlornly at its foot paws. Its curled tail drooped. "I was a gardener, but have been lost to my work. I need help to find my way back into the Gardens of Sweet Night."

Elroy laughed in spite of himself, spraying plum jack on his crossed legs and the grass in front of him. "A child's bedtime tale," he said, coughing up more plum jack, "and one with which to frighten bullies and cowards. A thousand pardons, but your jest is in poor taste."

The pug drew itself to its full seventy centimeters. "I do not jest. I know the way back to the Gardens, but it is not a road that I can travel alone. I can see I have wasted my time here. Good day, sir man."

"Wait, wait." Elroy stretched a hand toward the pug, palm outward. "I can see that you are serious about this fable. How is it that you plan to return?"

"Well," the pug sniffed. "It is an arduous journey, hence my need for a traveling companion. I have offered you a position of trust to travel at my side, if you will trust me to know where I am going."

Elroy nodded. "Your funds will stand me good stead when I return home. It is not my ambition to be a servant, but I will accept your wage. I am a human man called Elroy, and I will take your service."

"Friend Elroy, I accept your offer of service under the terms discussed. I am an Animal called Wiggles."

Elroy was profoundly glad he had no more plum jack in his mouth as he swallowed another laugh.

Somewhat Is Learned Concerning the Gardens

They walked toward New Dallas the balance of that day before settling down to rest under a baobab tree on a sparsely vegetated plateau. "*Adansonia digitata*," Wiggles identified the tree. "The South African baobab. They grow in rain shadows and drylands, as they do not favor too much water. The tree is not native to the Western Hemisphere. We are lucky it is not in fruit—they are notoriously rank."

The trunk of the tree was broad, like a wooden silo ramified with exposed roots, spreading to a great crown high above their heads. "I've never seen one," said Elroy. Baobabs did not grow around Pilot Knob.

"They can store one hundred tons of water. In their native ecosystems they serve as reservoirs that anchor dryland ecosystems. There is one in Babylon much larger, but that is the nature of things there."

Elroy waited politely for the pug to continue.

Wiggles sighed. "Babylon, one of the Gardens of Sweet Night." He scratched in the loam at their feet, drawing seven long ovals like sausages laid end to end. He pointed to them in turn.

"Heligan, Babylon, Suzhou, Eden, Daisenin, Gethsemane and Tuileries." His voice was sadness itself. "The green wealth of our Earth, captured and multiplied by the guiding genius of man and Animal."

"And you came from there?"

Wiggles nodded, a very manlike gesture. "Born and raised in Heligan."

"Why did you leave?"

The pug stared at Elroy, licking his own black face. "There was a misunderstanding. I was cast out for eating the apples of our Lord."

"Your Lord?"

"Liasis, High Commissioner of the Cis-Lunar Justiciary and Lord of Implementation for the Atlantic Maritime Territories."

Elroy had never heard of such a person. "Who is he?"

"The man who owns the world."

They watched the stars rise over the eastern horizon, the two of them stretched out together under the edge of the baobab's scattered branches. Venus came first, then Yurigrad, brightest of the thousand satellite stars, on its fast course through the sky.

"The stars shine like diamonds cold and hard in the skies that surround the Gardens," said Wiggles in a sleepy voice.

"This Liasis..." Elroy struggled with the name. "How does he own the world?"

The pug's tail thumped against the ground. "Do you pay taxes at home?"

"Me, no, but the village of Pilot Knob tithes every third moon."

Wiggles sat up, began grooming himself, tongue lapping through his fur. He stopped for a moment. "To whom does your village tithe?"

"The Travis Caldes."

Wiggles burrowed briefly into his groin. "And to whom do they in turn pay taxes?"

Elroy recalled his lessons in civics and economics. "I suppose they must pay them to the Republician government in Waco."

Another pause for air. "And to whom do the Republicians tithe?"

"I never imagined that they tithe anyone, sir pug. I did not know who might stand above them."

"Everybody tithes, in one fashion or another. And it all flows upward, friend Elroy. Only the Lord Liasis does not tithe. He and a few of his brethren."

"How can it be," wondered Elroy, "that if I am a free man, everything is owed to someone of higher station?"

"What does freedom mean?" Wiggles turned around several times and went to sleep.

The warmth of the new day washed over them. The baobab lay some kilometers behind. Elroy considered his bread crusts with longing as Wiggles spoke.

"I believe I can find a maglev station to speed us on our way to New Dallas. We will have far to go from there."

Old tutelage in archaeoscience tumbled through Elroy's memory. "Maglev. Magnetic levitation, yes? An ancient mode of rapid transport."

"Correct." Wiggles smiled while licking his nose. "Normally subterranean. This system was originally developed near the end of the First North American Ascendancy. As I recall, the La Grangians reconditioned it."

"I had no idea it was still active."

"Many things move above your head and beneath your feet of which you have never dreamed."

The discussion of last night still weighed on Elroy's mind. "How free am I?"

Wiggles laughed again. "You breathe of your own choosing, yes?"

"Yes, I suppose that I am free to breathe."

"Some people dwell in places where that is a right, licensed and paid for every turning of the moon. Yet they consider themselves free."

Elroy was shocked. "Free? When they must pay for the very air they breathe?"

"Some claim there is absolute freedom in holding responsibility for every aspect of their lives, including the air they breathe. Every day they live or die by the consequences of their actions."

Behind them a shrill blast from a steam whistle warned of an oncoming land train. Elroy and Wiggles left the road to stand in the twinned shadows of a honeysuckle that struggled over slow years to overwhelm a banyan tree.

"*Ficus benghalensis.*" Wiggles tapped a thick aerial root with a thumbed paw. "A relative of the mulberry, mistakenly thought by the ancients to be a fig tree. Another colonizer of these American shores. Traditionally, this tree represents shelter given by the gods, a symbol of their benevolence toward man."

The clanking, screeching land train overtook them, all brass piping, bright paintwork and great iron wheels. Elroy did not feel particularly sheltered.

Beset by Wolves, Any Man May Be a Hero

The land train groaned to a shuddering stop before their banyan tree. The sixth and final car halted directly in front of Elroy and Wiggles. Three security wolves jumped over the red and yellow ironwork sides, surprising them. One slammed Elroy back against the banyan tree using a rough arm across his chest while another knocked Wiggles down to pin him under a foot paw.

The lead security wolf leaned one forearm against the banyan tree while tapping Elroy on the chest with his staff. The wolf was definitely male, as were his gray and tan fellows. They all wore black armored vests. He growled through a toothy smile. "You two pups are in our crimebase, Freshmeat." The odor of his breath gagged Elroy.

Elroy was frightened, not for his life, but certainly for his safety, and that of Wiggles. Gathering his calm, he protested. "You don't even know our names. We have rights under the Mutual Contract."

"Rights." The lead wolf laughed, a very human sound. "I've heard of those." He leaned closer, the lolling tongue nearly swiping Elroy's nose.

"This little dog is a dangerous character, friend man. You'd do well to avoid his type." The wolf glanced down at Wiggles, squirming and whining on his back. "Breeding error, you know."

Elroy sized up the three wolves. Each stood taller than he, armed with iron-shod staves and stun guns. One was occupied standing on Wiggles, while the other two cornered Elroy against the aerial roots of the banyan. Bad odds, from a poor position, but he would not allow either fear or tactics to keep him from his responsibilities. His vows with the Little Brothers forbade attack, but defense was another matter entirely. Elroy centered himself as he had been taught, then drew a steady breath.

"Sir pug is my employer, and I owe him loyalty."

"Freshmeat, you don't listen well..." the security wolf began. Elroy spun a left snap kick that landed on the wolf's scrotum. Spinning through the kick, Elroy grabbed the staff as it tumbled from the shocked wolf's thumbed paw, following on to catch the next security wolf across the forearm.

The second wolf screamed as its ulna shattered. Elroy shoved the iron tip of the staff into the second wolf's chest, pushing it back into the banyan, before whacking the groaning first wolf alongside the head to keep it down. He turned to help Wiggles, only to see the pug with his jaws locked on the inner thigh of the third security wolf. That wolf shook Wiggles free and leapt on the pug, just as Elroy brought the staff down with a resounding thwack on the back of the wolf's head, pulling his blow so as not to kill.

Panting with adrenalin and relief, Elroy used the staff to lever the unconscious wolf off Wiggles.

"Sir pug, are you well?" he gasped.

"That bastard son of a beast smashed my phalanges," screeched Wiggles. "I fear I cannot walk, and more wolves are certain to come from the fore of the train."

It was terribly rare for a human to handle an Animal so, but Elroy scooped up the pug as his own breathing settled to a manageable rhythm. "Then this would be a fine time to remember where a maglev station might be."

He fled into the jungle, carrying the iron-shod staff in one hand and

Wiggles in the other. Elroy mumbled a prayer of thanks that he had not maimed or killed the security wolves.

They crouched in an understory deadfall on the jungle floor, listening for sounds of pursuit. The old rotted trunk was surrounded by large, flat leaves fallen from above, each the size of a serving platter. The leaves decayed with a gentle sugary smell.

Elroy's fear had been replaced by a rising sense of anger — at the situation, at the wolves, at Wiggles. "By the Cattle of the King, what was that ambush? My masters took my vow not to strike in anger, and already I am in default. I am paying dearly for your wage, sir pug."

"A moment, please," said Wiggles. "Allow me to collect my thoughts. You do fight very well for a peasant boy from the Texas jungles."

Elroy folded his hands and made a constrained bow within their sheltering greenery. "My spiritual masters practice an aggressively strenuous form of ethics. Now tell me, what brought the security wolves down on us?"

"Flaming Sword," said Wiggles. "The ones who cast me out. They guard the secrets of the Gardens of Sweet Night."

"The constabulary of your Lord Liasis?"

The pug drew himself to his feet with a groan. "The secret police, perhaps. Ancient tradition holds that a flaming sword bars the gates of the Garden of Eden, namesake of one of the Gardens of Sweet Night."

Elroy examined the staff. "I would expect the secret police to carry the fiercest of weapons."

"Not here, on the surface. It is forbidden by both common sense and the Mutual Contract. They expect no sharp resistance here. They will not make that mistake with us twice."

In the distance they heard the scream of the land train's steam whistle, long blasts in groups of three. Wiggles growled, his ears laid back flat. "They launch the search, as if we were dangerous brigands. Damned canids."

Elroy examined the jungle around them. His mind and body were calm again. "Well, then we must find your maglev station quickly. I presume it is hidden underground, or I would have heard of such a thing before." Elroy paused, working through his line of reasoning. "A maglev must use a lot of energy, and something that old would not be well shielded. Do you have a means of locating that kind of energy leakage?"

Wiggles looked surprised. "Excellent thinking, friend Elroy. You have been better tutored than I had hoped. I do have something like that, but to my embarrassment against all propriety you must again carry me. My foot paw pains me sorely."

Elroy scooped up the pug. "Show me the way." He trotted through the green-shadowed depths of the jungle floor, Elroy harboring regrets.

"Ware tigers, friend Elroy." Wiggles' voice was muffled against Elroy's shoulder.

"Surely you mean wolves?"

"No, I scent felids. Large beasts, not Animals. I understand that *Panthera tigris sumatrae* have become naturalized here in Texas."

"A wonder to behold, I am sure," Elroy replied, wondering how Wiggles could scent the difference between a beast and an Animal, "but I am ill equipped to stand off something larger and less foolish than your flaming wolves."

"If a tiger appears, I am confident you will think of something."

This stretch of jungle floor looked much like any other to Elroy, with dangling lianas and scattered deadfalls. Butterflies strayed down from the high canopy, drifting through isolated shafts of green-tinted sunlight.

After a time Elroy voiced his thoughts. "Between the tigers and the wolves, I worry if we will emerge from this jungle intact."

"Regretful you took my pay?"

"No." Elroy surprised himself. "The wolves attacked without warning, and offered no legal authority. Further, your money earns my way toward starting a family."

"Surely a thought worth a Justiciary penny." Wiggles gave another of his odd laughs. "Put me down here, please." He began snuffling around on all fours in a spiraled circle in the loam, limping to favor in his left foot paw.

"Here." Wiggles' voice carried from behind another banyan tree. "Bring that stick you have been carrying."

Elroy stepped around the tree to see Wiggles digging into the loam, scattering leaf mold and dirt behind him. He could hear Wiggles' thumbed paws scraped on something solid. The pug backed out of the hole, then stared up at Elroy. Elroy noticed the flowered waistcoat was as clean as it had been when he first met Wiggles—a sign of smart matter, although Elroy had never actually encountered the stuff before.

"Open it," suggested Wiggles.

Elroy peered into the hole. A metal hatch cover lay exposed about eight inches below the jungle floor, a large handle inset within a rounded recess. Elroy reached down with the iron-shod staff, levering it against the handle. He leaned with all his strength.

The handle did not budge.

"Harder," snapped Wiggles. Elroy noticed the pug's hackles were rising. He thought he could hear the distant echo of the steam whistle.

Elroy leaned against the staff, pulling with his entire weight, until his feet almost left the ground as the staff bent back.

The roar of a tiger startled him greatly.

The hatch handle screeched as it slid across the rounded recess. Elroy and the staff collapsed on Wiggles' dirt pile as Wiggles bounded to the sprung hatch and tugged at it with his thumbed paws.

The tiger roared again.

Elroy grabbed the hatch, pulling it wide open as Wiggles dove down the hole. Elroy tossed the staff after Wiggles and swung himself into the hole to the sound of a startled yelp from below. As he pulled the hatch cover closed, he saw the green eyes and tufted face of a Sumatran tiger peering in at him.

Wiggles' encouraging words echoed up from the darkness below. "Don't worry. It's the smallest species of tiger in the world."

A Magnetic Journey of Conscience to Flower Mound

They stood in a dimly lit hall, high-ceilinged and quite large. The echoes of Elroy's feet scuffling on cracked tile carried some distance. The whole area had a musty, oily smell, overlaid with the cool damp common to subterranean spaces. Vague reddish light from hidden sources obscured much more than it revealed.

Wiggles thumped his tail. "Excellent."

"Yes?"

"This was the Denton station. It is long out of commission as there is no town here anymore. The line still runs through it straight to our destination, however. I have already summoned a service car for a trip to Flower Mound, which you call New Dallas."

"So this is the maglev," whispered Elroy.

"Well, the station anyway. You will see the train soon enough."

They waited on a concrete bench in the silent dimness. Wiggles whimpered periodically from the pain in his paw. After a while Elroy realized their mistake.

"What will happen when the wolves discover the hatch?"

"First they will discover the tiger, I suspect." The pug snorted. "But in any case the dirt will have taken care of things by now. It isn't very bright, but it knows its job."

"The dirt?" Elroy realized Wiggles was an absolute oracle of lost technology. "Was it nanotechnology?"

"Exactly. Moderately intelligent nanodirt. It is self-restoring. That's what I looked for. We use it in the Gardens of Sweet Night. I have a detector sensitive to its signature."

When the maglev service car finally arrived, its running lights brightened the station. Elroy saw tall vaulted arches, cracked murals on the wall, and a row of long-shuttered shops. Tiny pairs of eyes gleamed in the shadows by the tunnel mouth.

The service car itself was an almost featureless polished wedge much different the steam-driven iron trains that Elroy had seen all his life, quiet as a stone. Elroy added disappointment to that day's catalog of emotions.

"Flower Mound." Wiggles stretched, shaking out his fur while licking his nose. "The lotus is a flower of great significance, symbolizing purity and divinity. These days people call this place New Dallas, but it is built on a most spiritual foundation."

"It is only New Dallas, sir pug, not the Vatican Aresian."

They stood in the Flower Mound maglev station. Similar in design to the abandoned Denton station, it was well lit, dressed stone walls bearing sculpted metal light fixtures. A tile mosaic floor supported scattered travelers seated on concrete benches or reading wall posters. The shops here were long-shuttered, too.

Elroy had left the iron-shod staff in the service car, as it seemed too conspicuous to carry through the station. He grumbled. "I walked all the way to the Glass Mountains while this world beneath could have carried me in swift comfort."

"But you were free every step of the way, yes?"

More free then than he was now, Elroy realized. "Are we much closer to the Gardens?"

"We are until the Flaming Sword picks up our trail," said Wiggles darkly. "Those wolves had no reason to carry nanosensors out there, but it won't take them long to reason out where we went. We must move onward and upward. Support me by clasping my thumbed paw, please. It would be a scandal for me to be seen riding in your arms."

Elroy extended a downward hand. "First, I suppose, we must find a way out of this station. Surely they do not employ a secret ladder here?"

"I am embarrassed to say that I feel enslaved by your wages." Elroy clutched the two Justies the pug had just given him, filled with a sense that he had surrendered control of his fate.

Wiggles smiled. "Freedom. An ideal of some concern to you. Consider that the meanest felon digging a ditch in restitution to his lord is a free man. He may place his mattock thusly or so at his own choice, bend or stand as he wishes."

Elroy leapt to the flaw in Wiggles' proposition. "Yet he is in chains, undeniably bound, his actions constrained."

"Those chains are of his choosing," said Wiggles. "The felon chose his crime, with the ditch as consequence. When I offered you service, you chose to join me. The Justiciary pennies in your hand and the pangs in your conscience are consequences. You are of course at liberty to resume your original journey."

They sat on a bench in the Gamelan Garden, a park in the center of New Dallas, just off Simmons Road. Wiggles had demanded rest in a cultivated park. He had declared Gamelan with its orchids and fleshy vines and vast bromeliads the palest imitation of the Gardens of Sweet Night, but still balm for his injured soul.

Elroy shook his head, studying the coins in his hand. "I will stay." He did not want to admit it, but Elroy was becoming fond of Wiggles.

"Caring is a surrender of freedom. You may see that I am trapped by my love of the Gardens, that this lovely *Odontoglossum hortensiae* so reminds me of." The pug sniffed at a pale, fleshy flower, his tail wagging. "Flowers are the mothers of insects, you know."

"Did they name it Flower Mound for the orchids that grew here?"

"Goodness, no." Wiggles laughed, his tail slapping the bench. "In those bygone days, what grew here were dryland plants such as prairie grasses, pecans and mesquite."

At Elroy's puzzled look, Wiggles added, "You know. *Prosopis glandulosa*. A nitrogen-fixer that anchored the boundaries of prairie." The pug rubbed his left foot paw with a thumbed paw. "My foot is sore hurt, friend Elroy."

Speaking the Language of the Sky

They stood in a line at the base of the mooring mast that towered above them, a slender blade of white metalloceramic stabbing into the sky toward the great bulk of the airship *Child of Crisis*. Elroy had seen dirigibles cruising above the trees all his life, as the usual airway from New Dallas to Monterey ran over Pilot Knob. He had never been close to one.

Elroy craned his neck to study the gondola at the bottom of the airship. It was doubtless quite large, but still appeared miniscule against the bulk of the gasbag. "I've never ridden the air before."

"To do so down here is of no comparison to the Gardens of Sweet Night."

"My experiences pale next to yours, sir pug," Elroy snapped, "but leave me the joy of what little I have to call my own."

"Peace, friend Elroy." Wiggles squeezed Elroy's hand, his small thumbed paw dry and stiff. "I did not mean to offend."

"Next load! Group six!" A red-faced young woman, her skin much paler than Elroy's woody brown complexion, shouted from the boarding doors at the base of the mast.

Wiggles checked his chits. "Let's go." The two of them shuffled through the hatch on to a small elevator with a number of other passengers. Behind them, Elroy saw the line of waiting people and Animals through the closing hatch.

The elevator hummed almost below audibility. Wiggles had warned Elroy about the sensation of being pushed down while the little car climbed the inside of the mooring mast. "I wish there were windows," Elroy whispered.

The car suddenly lurched, shaking in its rise. From the conductor's shocked gasp, Elroy gathered this was not part of the usual ride. They stopped for a moment, then began moving up again.

A bulging man with a thick, burred Mississippian accent sounded panicky. "And what would that have been?"

The conductor picked up a small handset from her control panel and listened. The car shuddered upward, much less smooth in its motion than before. Elroy could hear a deep groaning through the walls of the elevator.

They staggered to a stop and the doors hissed open to reveal a tiled floor about waist high to Elroy. The conductor dropped her handset. "There is a problem down below. The airship is casting off for its own protection. Please remain calm and stay in the elevator car."

"Flaming Sword," whispered Elroy. If they stayed in the elevator, the wolves would come for them, endangering the other passengers. He had to get away, to protect himself and everyone else. Elroy scooped Wiggles up in his arms like a beast and pushed toward the open doors.

"Here there, boy." The man with the Mississippian accent grabbed Elroy's arm. Elroy spun, swinging his elbow into the Mississippian's chest with a prayer for forgiveness. He had no time to reason with the man. Elroy miscalculated his blow and felt ribs crack.

"Moment of Inertia," Elroy wept through clenched teeth. "May the Little Brothers forgive me." He hopped one hip up onto the ledge that was the floor outside, and rolled out of the jammed elevator. The conductor plucked at his heel, but he ignored her.

The massive bulk of the *Child of Crisis* filled the sky above Elroy. Ahead of him it stretched into the distance, the shimmering metallic bulge of the airship's gasbag dropping below his view. The boarding platform at the top of the mast was about four meters square, while a slender spire arched up above him to meet a set of lines depending from the airship's nose. A narrow gangway about three meters long led to the open hatch of the gondola underslung along the forward curve of the airship.

Two sailors in crisp blue uniforms were unfastening the gangway from the open door, preparing to drop it loose. Wiggles whimpered as a series of explosions echoed up from the ground below. The platform swayed beneath Elroy's feet. There was no time for thought. He sprinted toward the gangway, screaming, "Wait, wait for us!"

One sailor looked up, the gangway's release chain slack in her hand. The other yanked his chain, causing the right side of the gangway to drop away from the hatch while the chains on the left took its full weight.

Elroy raced over the edge of the boarding platform onto the sagging gangway as the other sailor belatedly released her chain. Elroy pushed off as the gangway fell away, straining into the jump with Wiggles tucked firmly under his left arm. As he fell, Elroy reached forward with his right. It was like running the trees in his home jungle, only far more deadly.

The gangway tumbled away beneath his feet to swing from the boarding platform, revealing perhaps a hundred meters of empty air between Elroy and the flagged paving stones of the airfield. His fingers missed the hatch coaming, then grasped at the swinging chain as the second sailor hauled it in. Elroy caught the chain, but his body swung forward with the momentum of his jump and smashed against the gondola wall. Wiggles yelped, muffled by his arm.

As Elroy swung back on the chain, spinning over the airfield, he saw the boarding platform falling away from him. He realized the dirigible had cast off and now rose into the sky. People from the elevator were helping the bulky Mississippian on to the platform, while the conductor waved her fist at Elroy. Far below, he could see a fire at the base of the mooring mast, with figures struggling around it.

"Need a bit of help there, lad?" The female sailor peered down at him. Elroy spun slowly on the chain, grateful of the support wrapped around his forearm, even as the pressure of his weight threatened to crush his wrist within the chain's tightening grip. The two sailors peered from the open hatch above him.

"If you please," gasped Elroy. He wondered what the warm, acrid smell was, then realized he had pissed his pants.

"We'd need to see a boarding chit." The two of them grinned like monkeys sharing an armload of rotten papayas.

"A thousand pardons." Elroy shuddered. "I am somewhat constrained at the moment." He slipped two links down the chain, the length circling his wrist binding tighter. He could feel bones grind against one another. Elroy hissed with pain.

The woman pulled a serious face, rubbing her chin. "A right problem there, lad. Rules say we have to see the chit afore you can pass the hatch."

"Ancient law, that is," the second sailor added. "Protects everyone's rights, that does."

They both laughed.

Wiggles squirmed beneath his arm. "Money. Offer them money."

Elroy's hand slipped, and he felt an astonishing pain as his elbow threatened to come loose in its socket, counterpoint to the grinding in his wrist.

He clenched his teeth. "Perhaps a gratuity would be in order."

"Now you're speaking the language of the sky, lad." The two sailors hauled in their chain.

"Despite the irregularities of your embarkation, your boarding chits seem to be in order."

Elroy's wrist throbbed so severely that he had trouble focusing on the purser's words. They stood in the officer's abbreviated workspace in a forward cabin of the airship.

The purser was an aging golden retriever wearing a blue jacket with epaulettes. Its fur was braided in tight cornrows, each one clasped by a clip decorated with an ancient copper coin. It stared at Elroy and Wiggles as if they were unpleasantly spoiled cargo loaded by some error. "It seems I am stuck with you for now. What transpired back there at New Dallas?"

Wiggles glanced sidelong at Elroy, who took that as a hint.

"Sir purser," Elroy began. He was not sure what he should say, but he had brought them aboard the ship. He felt the way he had when summoned before the abbot for some infraction. "I am in service to this noble pug. We were chased by brigands. We thought to escape by boarding the *Child of Crisis*, but they were closer than we realized. My most humble apologies for bringing risk upon your vessel."

"Brigands," said the purser flatly. It stared at Elroy, its large brown eyes sweeping up and down his grimy beaded vest and torn muslin trousers. It then turned its gaze on Wiggles, whose green flowered waistcoat was, as always, immaculate.

"I may be a foolish old Animal who has spent his life among the free folk of the air, but I know brigands when I don't see them. Those were security wolves, firing indiscriminately down there with heavy weapons." It glanced at their boarding chits. "You two are fully paid and bound for Odessa Port. I've a mind to have you both tossed from the hatch to save me further trouble, but it's a fact that the Air Charter protects *Child of Crisis* and all her passengers and crew from precisely this harassment. Now tell me what you're really about."

Wiggles scratched his ear, then licked his nose. His tail stayed tight to his body as he spoke. "My servant and I are pursuing a quest."

"And that quest would be?"

Wiggles spoke with a quiet, proud strength. "Through error, I have been cast out of the Gardens of Sweet Night. I now make my way home."

The purser studied them a moment. "In their common room up against the belly of the gasbag, air sailors tell stories of those who die in the wide arms of the sky. Every man and Animal longs for a peaceful death in the air, followed by a sky burial. What we—they—say is that the bodies rise up singing into the heavens, until they come to the Gardens of Sweet Night. That is where they find their reward." It laughed, a stuttering bark deeper and richer than Wiggles' wheezing moments of humor. "Somehow you do not seem like one who has returned from the dark clouds of death."

"It is but truth, friend Purser. My story is as real as the Gardens themselves, for all that they may be myth to some."

"I do know more than the simple sailors."

"If you know the world," said Elroy unexpectedly, "you know injustice." He surprised himself with his words. "We have been pursued with a vengeance out of all proportion to any offense. You have your Air Charter. We have only our wits and our luck. I beseech your help in surpassing this wicked pursuit and gain entrance to the Gardens?"

"You speak well for a servant," said the purser, "As it happens, I have conceived of a way to lend a hand, spite the security wolves, and keep the *Child* from multiplying her current difficulties, all in one stroke. If I can persuade the captain to spite those who trespass on our ancient rights we may throw you from the hatch after all. Would you care to experience a sky burial of your very own?"

Rise Up Singing

The crew common room was low and dark, with a convex ceiling following the swell of the gasbag. Elroy, at two meters of height, could stand only along the slant walled sides where the ceiling reached up to about the top of his head. Long and narrow, with no windows and poor lighting, it felt to Elroy like the sarcophagus of some giant from prehistoric America.

"You effected our rescue quite well," said Wiggles.

Elroy snorted. "I assaulted an innocent man, then leapt into empty air, to be saved by dumb luck and a long chain."

"You saw what needed doing, and did it."

"Perhaps. But not now. What are we doing here?"

Wiggles rested in the hammock with Elroy, curled up against his side. One of the sailors had cleaned and bandaged his wounded foot paw, but the pain clearly bothered the pug.

"Hiding from passengers who will certainly be questioned at Odessa Port by the Flaming Sword. For the same reason the captain, too, cannot afford to see our faces."

"I know. I wondered about the sky burial. I am afraid of being tossed from the hatch."

"They will cast us out in a sort of flyer that is used to send out the dead. We will not plummet to the ground, but rather be rescued by secret friends."

Elroy still did not trust what was to come, but he had trouble imagining such an elaborate effort would be expended just to kill him. It couldn't be any worse than his leap onto the airship.

Elroy kept a wary distance from his rescuers, Nero and Mycroft, in the little storeroom where they were supposedly preparing his body. "You are *not* tying me to those splints. That's no flyer."

"Here, there," Nero said. "Your funeral is in ten minutes. You don't want to be late for it."

"Elroy," snapped Wiggles. "We do not have time for this."

"Look." Nero displayed a small bone-handled knife. "For later. To cut your way out. Trust us, you'll feel like a new man after your funeral."

Elroy stepped over to the splints. They were body length, cross-braced to a large capsule of a dull-colored matte plastic. Nero had given him a blue uniform jacket, without epaulettes, while Mycroft stood by with a winding sheet for the 'corpse.'

"Wiggles..." Elroy began. Control of his situation kept slipping further away from him.

The Animal licked his own nose, then grasped Elroy's hand with a thumbed paw. "We must, friend Elroy. This will work."

Elroy lay down with the greatest reluctance and allowed Nero to bind him to the splints. The straps came across his upper arms, leaving his forearms free from the elbow down—not restraints, exactly. Nero slipped the bone-handled knife into Elroy's right hand. Wiggles crawled between Elroy's legs, where he was enclosed in the winding sheet that Mycroft wrapped from Elroy's feet to his waist. The sheet was some sandpapery weave of sackcloth cheaply printed with block patterns of birds soaring among blazing stars.

"Oh are you in for a treat. While we're in the cargo hold, try to remember you're dead," Mycroft whispered in Elroy's ear. "Don't breathe where the passengers might see you."

Nero and Mycroft hoisted the splint ends and carried Elroy as if on a stretcher into the aft cargo hold of the *Child of Crisis*. Eyes slitted open, Elroy could see through his lashes an honor guard of four sailors to one side of the great double doors of the aft cargo hatch. Two of them played a fast-paced dirge on an electric sackbut and an out-of-tune finger harp. The musical effect was unique in Elroy's experience.

The purser stood in front of the hatch doors with a small book in its hand. Nero and Mycroft lowered Elroy onto the deck, the capsule beneath the splints taking his weight. Elroy could hear a rustle of people behind his head, presumably passengers and crew in attendance of his funeral rites.

"Crew, passengers, the ship our mother," intoned the purser. "I beseech all to draw near and take comfort." It made vague motions with the book in its thumbed paws.

"In accordance with the rules of the Air Charter first granted us by the counselors of La Segunda Republica Norteamericana in years of lost history, and further in accordance with the timeless rites of the Brotherhood of the Sky, we gather today to commit to a sky burial the mortal remains of able airman third class Vulpen, born of the airship *Fortune's Enemy*, and in service on the *Child of Crisis* since his seventh year. As our customs dictate, the remains of airman Vulpen will be cast out into the air for a sky burial, that his soul might guide him upward to the Gardens of Sweet Night where he may find his eternal reward."

Elroy moaned, very quietly. He was supposed to cut the bonds with the knife in his hand, but where was the promised flyer? Elroy began to sweat.

The purser continued. "The Captain has taken us up above the clouds so that airman Vulpen's soul may rise up singing into the glorious light of the day star, bearing his mortal remains to that which awaits him. As I open the hatch doors, I ask everyone to bow their heads in respect for the dead."

"You're on," Mycroft stage-whispered. Through his slitted lids, Elroy watched two of the honor guard crank open the hatch doors while the other two wheezed and tootled their way through some airmen's paean. A sharp draft of very cold air swirled in as Mycroft added, "Don't cut too soon, friend."

Mycroft and Nero ran forward, dragging Elroy with them. The purser's smiling face flashed by with a wink and a pained squeal from the electronic sackbut, then Elroy launched into the air.

He described a long arc down from the airship, screaming with every gram of his strength as the rumpled clouds below him grew larger and larger.

In the Belly of the Orange Balloon

A crack like the snapping of a mighty tree trunk interrupted Elroy's prolonged terror. Within the winding sheet, Wiggles nipped at his calves.

Their free fall pulled abruptly short, slamming Elroy into the straps that held his body. The one across his shoulders slipped to his neck, nearly strangling him as it bruised his larynx. Improbably, he still held on to the knife.

His fall turned into a gentle trembling flight above the clouds. Elroy lay face down, pulled against the straps by his own weight. Wiggles struggled against the winding sheet, threatening to break through and resume his own, independent fall.

Elroy found his voice well enough to snap at Wiggles. "Stop moving, sir pug." To his surprise, he was no longer screaming.

Elroy craned his neck, trying to look over his shoulder. Above him to each side was a large, orange fabric wing with jointed skeletal ribs, like the wings of the flying foxes of his home forest in Pilot Knob. Elroy heard a steady hissing noise distinct from the flapping of the air across the fabric wings.

"Something is happening."

"What?" demanded Wiggles, who had wrapped all four paws around Elroy's left leg.

"We are no longer falling, and something is hissing above us, between our new wings."

"This is the whole point of a sky burial." Wiggles' voice was muffled by Elroy's legs and the winding sheet. "We're in an orbital drop-up pod."

"This is the flyer?"

"Yes. It flies to orbit. We're heading back to the Gardens."

Elroy watched as a great balloon slowly spun itself into being around them.

They sat on the floor of the balloon, propping the splints across its inner curve for something to lean against. Opaque, about five meters in diameter, the balloon enveloped them in a diffuse orange light leached from the sunny sky outside.

Elroy had used the knife to cut them away from the splints. He then carefully tucked it in the pocket of his uniform jacket. His wrist, strained from their embarkation of the dirigible, caused him excruciating pain. Seeking something else on which to focus, Elroy noticed that the inside of the balloon carried a sharp chemical odor, redolent of freshly milled plastic with a metal undertone.

Wiggles watched Elroy sniff. "Nanotrace is what you smell. You know, that knife won't harm this balloon."

"Neither will it harm me, now that I have put it away, sir pug." Elroy hugged his legs. He was cold, shivering, and he felt very lost.

"You have lost your nerve. You suffer from shock, I think." Wiggles scooted next to Elroy, curled his small body against Elroy's side.

"Nerve?" Elroy tried to laugh, succeeding only in producing a dry cough. "I will never have nerve again. The Green Man help me if I ever so much as hop from a log. I want to go home."

"You are going home. We're going back to the Gardens. They are the true home of every person, balm for the soul and liniment for the body."

"A plague on your Gardens." Elroy stifled a sob. "I nearly fell to both our deaths in New Dallas, then again just now. We are floating through the sky in an orange bubble, I am hungry but my stomach threatens never to take food again, and I have to piss somewhere in this empty ball. I miss my quiet treehouse in Pilot Knob. I have had enough of your quest."

Wiggles was silent for a while, his tail thumping gently against the fabric of the balloon. Elroy heaved and choked through tearless sobs, burying his face in his knees. After a time he stopped, only to stare at his orange tinted hands.

"You're going to the sky, Elroy," Wiggles finally said. "You will walk in the Gardens of Sweet Night and learn the true meaning of wonder."

"I'd like to learn the true meaning of a hole to piss in."

"Just urinate on the fabric of the balloon. It's very smart. It will carry the urine away and break it down for raw materials."

"Why does the waist of the balloon sometimes flatten widely, then contract to a ball again?" Elroy had been watching the orange walls for quite some time.

"I believe it makes more, then less of an airfoil."

"Airfoil..." Elroy mused. "That means wing, right?"

"Yes, friend Elroy. A lifting body." They were again curled together at the bottom of the balloon. The purser, or perhaps the sailors, had thoughtfully included a package of supplies at the back of the stretcher. Elroy ate sparingly of a waxed packet of airship flat bread. He had no great desire to see what the skin of the balloon might do with his shit. The urine processing had been sufficiently alarming.

"The balloon," the pug continued, "rides air currents and thermals to the highest altitude it can reach in that manner. It is a very clever machine, in its limited way. Once it decides it will profit no further from soaring the middle atmosphere, it will commence a steady low-power jet burn fueled by conversion of atmospheric gases. We will feel that as a slow push downward. At some point, when it has gained sufficient altitude from that procedure, somewhere in the upper atmosphere, the final motor, a flat fission device, will boost us into low orbit. The process can take several days, but it is quite efficient, and therefore cheap. Especially as the balloon is reusable."

Elroy shook his head, straining to believe. "Orbit. In space around our Earth."

"Yes. In the high places, where the Gardens of Sweet Night sweep forever about the mother world."

Wiggles made Elroy don the flimsy silver suit he found in the purser's package. There was a smaller suit, more of a bag with a head at one end, for Wiggles. The pug explained. "Survival suits. Simple space suits, really, although quite dumb for space equipment. Now that we are boosting toward orbit the balloon cannot protect us from the extreme cold."

"They cannot possibly bury their dead in the air this way," said Elroy. "This technology is costly and complex."

"Senior officers are sent off this way. Crewmen such as the late airman Vulpen are normally sent out the hatch with a small sounding balloon, enough to keep them in the air for a few days."

"I have never found a dead airman on the ground."

"How many airmen die each day? How big is the ground? I also would imagine the Brotherhood of the Sky is considerate of where they perform their rites."

Elroy mused on the Brotherhood of the Sky. "Now, they were free."

"Free because they travel about?"

"Yes." He imagined life on an airship, seeing the great cities of the world from high above, immune to wars, to floods and fires, avoiding famines and pestilence.

"It is unlikely Nero or Mycroft have ever set foot on soil. Remember how high the mooring mast was in New Dallas?"

"I assumed it was a safety measure."

Wiggles shook his head, licking his nose. "The Air Charter was written to cover aerial operations of ground-based organizations. Now, the airships are in perpetual flight. If they were to land, and the Justiciary could catch them on the ground, the crews would forfeit property and freedom. Born in the air, they are citizens of nowhere and tithe no one. They have no rights at all on the ground."

"So they are free, but not to walk the forests or swim the rivers."

"Free within their domain, but absolutely restricted to it."

Elroy thought about the massive bulk of the *Child of Crisis*. "If the airships never touch the ground, where are they built?"

"In orbit, where different laws and regulations apply. The airships are

147

built in space, and lowered with massive orbital drop-down pods, analogous to orbital drop-up pods like this one."

"So they pay for their ships by smuggling goods or funds back to space in these orbital drop-up pods."

Wiggles barked his short, odd laugh. "I appreciate a young man with a keen grasp of economics."

"They must bury a lot of officers. Some of them many times over."

"I am given to understand their death rate is uncommonly high on occasion," Wiggles said in his most serious voice.

Nighttime in the Light of the Day Star

The heavier thrust finally eased. Elroy felt himself floating off of the floor of the balloon. He and Wiggles both wore the thin silver suits, enclosing even their heads, the hoods having transparent panels across the face. Elroy tried to move, but instead began to spin. His head began to spin with the roiling in his gut.

Wiggles' voice echoed tinny and thin within Elroy's silver hood. "Have a care, friend Elroy. We are in microgravity, often called weightlessness. It can be dangerous and distressing to a newcomer."

Elroy grabbed for a splint, but succeeded only in knocking it into a spin as well. He needed to talk, to focus his mind on something other than the distress of his body. "We have been in this balloon for two or three days, sir pug. I am very tired of the view, no offense. What happens now?"

Wiggles wagged his short tail, visible by the rippling in his silver space suit. "Friends of the purser will come for us soon."

"Does it ever happen that the Flaming Sword or other agents of the Lord Liasis find these drop-up pods?"

"Yes."

Elroy had been thinking about Wiggles, about the wages he took and the choices that had been forced upon him. The balloon shuddered, and he found himself pressed against the fabric of the balloon. Elroy realized that the pain in his wrist had subsided quite a bit.

Wiggles kicked off, sailing in his silver suit to be next to Elroy. "We have been taken in tow. Let us hope for friends."

"How will we know?"

"Friends will stow the balloon gently for future use. Enemies most likely will force their way in."

"Wiggles," said Elroy. "When we are released, by friend or foe, I will stand with you, but I will be your servant no longer."

Wiggles gave Elroy a long, thoughtful look. "Why?"

"I am not made for service. I do not need the funds so badly as to surrender myself. Since we boarded the airship, every choice has been taken from my hands. I will stand beside you and help you get back to the Gardens, not for payment, but for friendship."

"Thank you, Elroy. I hope you can leave your regrets behind as we continue."

Pressed against the fabric with Wiggles, Elroy watched for signs of civilized entry.

They came soon enough. The balloon suddenly stopped. Elroy and Wiggles collapsed to the new floor that had been the wall at their back, drawn down again as if they were back on the ground. The orange fabric rapidly lost tension as it settled around them. With a gentle sussing noise it began to tighten in on itself.

One of the fabric panels split open above them, the rangy brindled face of a badger peering in. It wore a canvas work vest. "Ho, new friends. Is there cargo to be recovered?"

Wiggles unsealed his silver hood, motioning Elroy to do the same. As his hood opened, Wiggles spoke. "We are a special shipment, sir badger, courtesy of the *Child of Crisis*."

"Always looking out for us up here in the high places, that Renton. A great purser and a better person, but can't resist sending us little surprises from time to time." The badger pushed and nudged at the collapsing fabric of the balloon to open an exit for them.

"I am Wiggles, a gardener from the high places, and this is my friend Elroy of Pilot Knob, Earth."

The badger nodded gravely at Elroy. "Pilot Knob is a place I've never heard of, but coming in this pod you've visitor's rights. Be welcome. And you, sir Wiggles. Are you truly just a simple gardener?"

"With respect, I decline the question pending further discussion, sir badger."

"Which says enough about the special shipment. You may call me

Horace. We must go now. By virtue of the method of your arrival, you have been summoned to a Concilium meeting."

They stepped out of the shrinking balloon into a large bay reminiscent of the rear cargo bay of the *Child of Crisis*, except everything here was ceramic, plastic or metal. Elroy was fascinated by the profusion of colored pipes, thick cables, and cabinets, with small doors and cunning hatches everywhere.

Horace led them to a hatch two meters tall, obviously intended for human foot traffic. Elroy paused to look at a small glass panel the left of the door. He stared at the tiny lights that crawled across the panel until the great blue arc of the Earth swung into his view.

"Welcome to space," said Wiggles.

Elroy reached out to touch the panel. It was cold. He felt his sense of wonder unfolding like flowers in the spring. "Why does the man who owns the world live up here high above?"

Wiggles barked a soft laugh. "Where else would you find such a view?"

The badger tugged at Elroy's silver sleeve, urging him along.

They passed through several short, winding corridors, lined with the same riot of pipes, cables, and access hatches as the cargo bay. To Elroy's nose the place smelled painfully clean. It had an aseptic, neutral scent impossible to achieve in an organic environment. Horace stopped them outside a double hatch emblazoned with a stylized paw print.

"Here is the Concilium. I counsel respectful attention, and the best kind of honesty in answering their questions."

The doors hissed open before them. At a gentle push from Horace, Elroy and Wiggles stepped into the room.

Elroy gasped. For a panicked moment, he thought he had stepped into open space. The Concilial chamber was roofed with a transparent dome, eight meters in diameter and open to half the sky. The great blue and white arc of the planet Earth was nowhere to be seen, but the room was flooded with the light of the sun, the daystar. All around his head, Elroy could see stars great and small, many of them in motion, like Yurigrad seen from Earth.

He pulled his gaze from the sky to the Concilium. Variously seated and standing about a low, round table almost three meters across, eight Animals stared at him. There were no human people in the room except for Elroy. He saw four dogs of varying breeds, including another pug, as well as a raccoon, two coyotes and a puma that bulked large along one arc of the room. As with every Animal, all wore a single item of clothing to symbolize their work or rank. Every vest or jacket or waistcoat was as unnaturally clean as the one Wiggles wore.

The Concilium pug leaned forward, drumming its claws on the metal tabletop. "Wiggles."

"Clement," Wiggles acknowledged. Elroy glanced down to see Wiggles sag his shoulders, tail drooping.

"A gardener, indeed." Clement's voice oozed reproach. "Who had you hoped to deceive?"

"*I am* a gardener, Clement."

"And a great deal more besides. In light of your misdeeds, our Lord Liasis is much inflamed with hope of hearing news of you."

"You are free Animals here." Wiggles turned his head, staring from one Conciliator to another. "Liasis is not Lord of places such as this. The Mutual Contract does not hold sway above the soil of Earth."

The puma rumbled a low growl. Elroy had never seen such a large Animal. It was greater in size and apparent ferocity than even the security wolves. "Clement misspoke. Liasis is not our Lord, but he is yours, sir Wiggles. We are good neighbors, and seek to satisfy his reasonable requirements."

Wiggles nodded. "In return for reasonable rewards, perhaps, friend puma?"

The puma licked a thumbed paw. "It is the way of things, little dog. Your sun now sets."

Clement stared up at Elroy. "You, friend Elroy, are free to go. Horace will escort you to the airlock."

Wiggles waved Elroy back with a small gesture of one thumbed paw. Elroy reached out to touch Wiggles, thinking perhaps to pull him along. The badger grabbed Elroy's hand, whispering, "Come quickly, man, while they still allow."

The doors of the Concilial chamber began to hiss shut upon Elroy's view of Wiggle's green-clad back. Beyond his friend the pug, Elroy saw the puma rising and turning to come toward Wiggles. Wiggles' head was bowed, his tail almost slack in its unkinked dejection, as the paw print doors closed.

Horace led Elroy rapidly through a series of cluttered corridors. Elroy stalked behind the badger, angry and confused.

"By the Moment of Inertia, what was that business? I will not allow a friend to be so betrayed!"

"Peace, friend Elroy. The Concilium is constrained."

"But that—Clement, Clement knew Wiggles. It said a few choice words, and Wiggles just stood there. After all we went through to come this far."

The badger stopped, turned to face Elroy, staring up at his human height. "Clement and Wiggles are littermates. Each chose a different path in life. Wiggles has deviated from his path, and Clement seeks to right perceived wrongs."

Littermates? "This is about the apples in the gardens then? A touch of brotherly jealousy?"

"You know nothing of what happens here in the high places, man from Earth, let alone the Gardens of Sweet Night. Wiggles was chancellor to Lord Liasis—a high official of the Justiciary in his own right."

Chancellor? Elroy leaned back against the corridor wall, pipes pressing into him. His worldview shifted underneath him like the falling gangway above New Dallas. He had no conception of what he should do next.

Horace tapped a claw upward into Elroy's chest, emphasizing his next words. "The Concilium was threatened, challenged for orbital rights and various alleged violations of law and charter. Wiggles worked secretly to defend Clement's interests, tried to make things smooth. In doing so, he betrayed the trust of his Lord Liasis. Fear of Liasis was stronger than loyalty to his brother, so Clement reported Wiggles to the Flaming Sword. From this came his fall."

"For brother to betray brother..."

"You have an appointment with the airlock. The Concilium has declared you free to go."

Stepping Into the Sunlit Dark
Horace led Elroy to a man-sized hatch set in a wide spot in a corridor. Another window stood next to it, showing the lights of the stars, both

moving and still.

"Here is the airlock you should use, friend Elroy."

Elroy stared out the window. "What is out there?"

"Space."

"I mean, where I am I going?"

"Space."

Elroy sputtered. "That's ridiculous. I would die."

The badger pushed a button, causing the hatch to open. "Then it is a lucky thing that you seem to be wearing a space suit. I should seal my hood were I you."

Elroy considered fighting the badger, rebelling against the order, but to what point? It was the Concilium's home, they certainly had security to deal with him. He would only harm Horace, who had been kind. With a sigh, Elroy stepped into the small room behind the airlock, pulling the silver hood back over his head.

"This is it? I am just to step out into the sun-drenched dark to die? I have come all this distance to meet my end? This is senseless."

Horace gave him a long look that seemed almost sympathetic. "There is a deeper game in play here. Trust that you will be alone, but not friendless."

Elroy watched the hatch slide closed as he sealed his hood. The soft silver suit crinkled around him, expanding and tightening in different places at the same time as a hissing sound began, first as almost a roar before trailing off to nothing. The floor released its hold on him, and Elroy drifted slightly away from it. He felt the same absence of direction they had felt in the drop-up pod.

Weightless, Elroy kicked his way out of the other end of the open airlock, into the depths of orbital space. It seemed expected of him.

I have finally found true freedom, thought Elroy. I am free of everything. Free of weight, free of responsibility, free of action of any kind.

Elroy's experiences in the orange balloon helped him keep his stomach and his mind anchored in place as he spun gently away from the rambling assemblage of the Concilium's high place in the sky.

He had never asked what their charter was, whose Council they were. Perhaps they spoke for all the Animals. He wondered what Horace had meant by deeper games. The business in the Concilium chamber had seemed almost rehearsed, a play perhaps. Who was being fooled? Wiggles? Elroy himself?

Earth rolled by his vision, transiting like a drunken giant. He noticed two kinds of stars, the sharp, far ones that didn't move except as he did, and the blobby, bright ones that moved at many speeds in many directions. The moving group must be the satellite stars, places such as Yurigrad. Perhaps they were other high places, or other adventurers like himself. Elroy felt his pulse echo in his ear. He was very, very far from Pilot Knob. The sunlit face of Earth showed the far side of the planet, so he could not even find his home.

"I suppose I shall die here," he said aloud as he began again to pray for the harm he done, to the security wolves and the unfortunate Mississippian. He prayed for the family he would never have, and prayed for Wiggles.

Horace's voice echoed in his ears, from inside the silver hood. "Not if you listen to what I tell you."

Suit radio, Elroy realized. "You have interrupted me at prayer, sir badger. Are we playing your deeper game now?"

"There is little time," snapped the badger. "Many things are not right at the moment, and you would do well to listen. I can help you help Wiggles. That great oaf Alcindor the puma even now sets out to return friend pug to his angry master. Can you see our station?"

Elroy waited with a smile for the Conciliatory home to spin into view.

"Yes, I see it now."

"Watch for a departure. Alcindor is about to set out in a maintenance sled with Wiggles. I have gained control of his autolaunch processes. I will direct the sled to pass very close to you. It will trail a line. You must grasp that line and secure yourself to the sled."

Elroy's smile broadened as the station rolled away from his view. The importance of everything diminished like a rock down a well. "Perhaps I shall grasp a shooting star as it trails by, friend Horace. I thank you for your kindness."

He yawned, a great gape that threatened to enclose his nearly dreaming mind.

"Sparks and fire," swore the badger. "Your oxygen is running low. Listen, friend Elroy, attend quickly. This is a maintenance sled. There are consumable service points at the base of the sled body. If you warp yourself in along the line, you may be able to steal air from its service reserves. I can intercept his telemetry and feed false data to keep Alcindor from wondering about the wallow from your added mass. Find the sled, steal air, and ride it in pursuit."

Elroy hummed, then sang. "I shall steal thunder from the storm and fly with the lightning."

In his ears, Horace sounded sad. "Good-bye, friend man. I have tried. Luck to you."

Elroy watched the blue Earth spin slowly by, thrilled by the patterns of the clouds.

"Now, Elroy, now!"

He couldn't remember the voice, couldn't see anyone, but as Elroy blinked he saw a silver line swinging toward him. Like swinging down the lianas of his jungle home, he thought, although he could see no green. His ears told him that he was falling, so he grabbed the silver liana to stop himself.

Black spots moved before Elroy's eyes, obscuring his view of the dark beyond. The silver vine yanked at his wrist, renewing an old, forgotten pain, but it restored his sense of upwardness. He looked at his feet, seeing a great house of metal far below, impossibly shaped and larger than any estate had a right to be.

The Concilium.

Elroy remembered a dog named Wiggles, a friend and boon companion. Wiggles was in trouble, needed Elroy's help.

Elroy climbed the silver vine, noting that it lacked leaves. He wondered why he was surrounded by the night, above, behind and below him. After a while the vine ended in an irregular wall of metal. There seemed to be an inordinate number of small cubes, pipes and metal balls. Elroy grabbed a sturdy pipe, releasing his silver vine.

In front him, Elroy found a row of taps, little serrated cones topped with colored handles. Each colored handle was labeled—'N_2H_4' was red, 'H_2' was orange. A blue tap handle read 'H_2O.'

He needed air. H_2O was water. H_2 was hydrogen. His vision began to black out as Elroy found a white tap handle labeled 'O_2.' Air, or at least oxygen.

He turned the white tap handle. Pale fog jetted out of the tip below the handle, disappearing almost immediately into a crystal spray, which then vanished. Air, apparently, but how was he to breathe it?

Elroy's stomach felt tight, as dark and uninterested as his mind was becoming, but he fingered the closure of the silver hood. Elroy could imagine the effects of vacuum on his skin and eyes. So first he tried to kiss the tap through his silver hood. To his surprise, the hood slipped onto the tap, pulling his face right up to the maintenance sled.

He turned the tap, feeling the jet of gas swelling his hood and pushing into his mouth with a sensation like drinking from a well-shaken bottle of ale. The black spots in his vision went away and Elroy began to giggle. His ears thrummed.

Elroy felt very alive, very fine, sliding among the tiny stars.

Into the Gardens of Sweet Night

"Wake up, boy."

The smell was natural, like real air. Elroy knew that he wasn't in the Concilium's high place any more. He could smell soil, plants, open water. And close by, the musky scent of large canids.

Elroy opened his eyes. A tall, lanky human, with skin as pale as a jungle puffball, leaned over him. Two security wolves flanked the man, clad in armored vests and carrying matte black energy pistols gleaming with tiny colored status lights. One of the wolves leaned over to stare into Elroy's face. "Will he survive?"

"There may be some residual effects from the oxygen overdose." The pale man stood up, favoring Elroy with a sad smile as he turned to leave the room.

"Won't matter much longer." Both wolves laughed, full human sounding laughs through their long toothy jaws. "Come on, boy, it's time for your confession."

They pulled Elroy to his feet, almost dropping him to the floor as he slid off the exam table. Elroy stumbled with them, a thumbed paw gripping each of his arms far too tightly.

"Where are we?"

"Heligan." The wolf to his left snickered. "Some of us will live to enjoy it."

Heligan. One of the Gardens of Sweet Night. Elroy looked around as the wolves yanked him into a corridor. The hallway was carpeted and paneled with dark hardwoods, like the public halls of the monastery of the Little Brothers of High Impact. Nothing at all like the metal burrows of the Concilium.

"Where are the plants?" He stared at the wooden walls with brass hand grabs punctuating them.

The security wolves laughed again, both relaxing their grip as they walked. The left one, the apparent spokesman, flexed the claws of his thumbed paw into Elroy's arm, puncturing skin even through the silver suit. Elroy could feel blood welling inside his sleeve.

"You'll be seeing them from inside the soil soon enough. Our Lord Liasis likes the freshest fertilizer."

The time had come for defense, Elroy realized. The vows he had taken, then broken in Wiggles' service, would never require him to go meekly to his death.

The knife was still in his jacket pocket, unreachable beneath the silver space suit. Elroy found his center, as he had learned in the Glass Mountains of Oklahoma. His perception of time stretched, each footfall on the carpeted floor like the slowest of drumbeats.

If he accepted a ragged wound in his right arm from the clawed grasp of his captor, he could bring that arm at full swing across the chest of the wolf to his left, while moving his left hand still inside the other wolf's grip to close both hands in the rib smashing technique the Little Brothers called "Kitten and Ball." He had learned at the land train that security wolves could be fought like men.

The Little Brothers taught that plan was thought, thought was action, action was deed. Elroy slumped to the left, then spun on that heel into the grip of the lead wolf. He pulled his right arm against the loose set of the right hand wolf's claws, gaining the painful ragged wound he expected, joining its pain to that of his bruised bones.

Increasing his spin, Elroy brought his right arm across the chest of the wolf, twisting his body so the flat of his left hand could provide counterpressure to the coming blow. With a crunch of collapsing ribs, the surprised wolf faltered in his step, allowing Elroy to break free on that side and spin around.

As the injured wolf fell, his partner swung the black energy pistol up to fire it at Elroy. Elroy finished his spin, slipping into a snap kick that threw the energy pistol upward in the grip of the second wolf. Shoulder first, Elroy slammed into the second wolf's chest as a violet bolt of light struck the wooden ceiling of the hall. The wood above him charred as Elroy drove the wolf backward into the wall. Elroy grabbed the wolf's armored vest at the left lapel, using it to slam the wolf against the wall.

The vest slipped off the wolf's torso and down its arm as the Animal spun. Elroy fell away, surprised, clutching the vest so that it was ripped entirely off the security wolf. His momentum carried him to carpeted floor, next to the weakly kicking foot paws of the first wolf. As fire alarms screamed above his head, Elroy tensed for a counterstrike from the second wolf.

It slumped against the wall, whining and whimpering. Elroy saw a braided silver strand dangling down its back, emerging from the fur at a point several vertebrae below the joining of neck and shoulder. He flipped the vest over in his hand.

Torn silver filaments on the inner side of the vest matched the strand. The wolf muttered, dropped to all fours and began to stagger away, gun, vest, and Elroy forgotten.

Elroy shrugged on the vest, which fit him loosely, then grabbed one of the energy pistols. The first wolf rolled to look up at him as Elroy aimed the pistol at its head.

"You will never escape my Lord Liasis." The security wolf grinned through pained gasps. Elroy could barely hear him over the din of the alarms.

"I don't plan to." Unwilling to pull the trigger, to kill a weakened enemy, Elroy reversed the energy pistol. He smashed the butt into the side of the wolf's head. It slumped onto the carpet, still breathing.

Elroy left the other security wolf's vest alone. He walked down the hall past the wolf's creeping, whining fellow, humming a battle hymn from the Little Brothers in counterpoint to the whooping fire alarms.

He wondered how to find Wiggles.

Elroy ducked through several hatches until he found a maintenance closet in which to rest. He had begun to tremble in the aftermath of the fight. The whooping fire alarms were an increasingly distant wail, and Elroy had the cold sweats.

He laid his energy pistol against one of the lockers in the closet, rested his hands on his knees and took a deep, shuddering breath. He had trained with the Little Brothers to acquire focus and strength, not to render Animals into beasts.

"Detachments moving within fifty meters," whispered a flat voice from his collar.

Elroy jumped, slamming his head against a locker. He twisted around, seeing the bunched silver hood of his suit overlaying the paneled black of the armor vest.

"Do you wish to evade?" It was the voice inside his hood again.

"Horace? Wiggles?"

"Status unknown." There was a brief crackling noise. "Tactical interface feed is being conducted through your suit communications."

Elroy felt a sharp prickle of fear. "Are you the vest?"

"Cognitive prosthetic, canid, combat, model one seventeen bis."

Robust technology, thought Elroy. It made sense. Every Animal he had ever seen wore a single item of clothing on their upper body. Elroy had always thought it was to emphasize their differentiation from beasts. With the size of most of their brain cases, Animals must store portions of their consciousness in these things.

"I want to find Liasis," he said. Where Liasis was, he would find Wiggles as well.

The vest whispered, "Exit this locker, proceed twelve meters to your left and pause. I will direct you from there."

Elroy grabbed his pistol, stepped out of the hatch and proceeded twelve meters to his left.

The vest guided him down corridors and through access tubes that climbed up and down. As the vest tracked the location of wandering security wolves, it told Elroy to make sudden pauses, and sometimes changed instructions even as he moved.

Elroy thought to ask it if he was visible to other vests.

"This unit has a tracer function."

How strange that the other security wolves had not yet used it to track him. Elroy was beginning to feel very set up. "Can you turn it off?"

159

"Disable tracer is a priority four order. Do you have priority four authority?"

Wiggles. Wiggles was supposedly Chancellor, or had been. "Chancellor Wiggles ordered me to help him."

"Tracer disabled."

Wiggles, it seemed, still had a name to conjure with.

"What else can you do?"

"Level one help is available. Options are: armor characteristics, biometrics, canid interface, cognitive extension, external communications, maintenance, memory and storage, miscellaneous settings, product specifications, shielding, smart matter, stealth, tactical support, weapons interfacing, user preferences. Please specify your desired path."

Elroy sighed. It was far more complex a technology menu than he had time to deal with. "Never mind. Just keep telling me how to find Liasis."

"Wait thirty-five seconds, then open the hatch to your right and proceed downward two levels."

Elroy counted to thirty-five, then opened the hatch.

The vest whispered through his open hood. "Once you exit this service tunnel, proceed left thirty meters and you will be before Liasis' audience chamber. Enter the chamber and you will be free to proceed to target."

Elroy was moved by an impulse he couldn't define, rooted in a vague belief that anything that spoke must have desires of its own. "I don't need to take you in there."

"Where else would I go?"

"I could take you off, leave you here. You would be safe, free." Even as he said it, Elroy felt foolish.

The vest made the static noise again, several times in a row. Elroy wondered if that was its thinking noise or its laughing noise.

"I am a cognitive combat prosthetic. I am an item of clothing for an Animal. What does freedom mean to me?"

"You know enough to ask that question," Elroy pointed out.

More static, then silence. Elroy waited, listening for noises behind the door. He heard none.

"There are four security wolves in front of Liasis' chamber," the vest finally whispered. "If you are prepared, you can overwhelm them with your energy pistol."

"And you?"

"I will come. If you win free again, I will still be with you."

"I'm not going to make it, am I?"

"In order to avoid panic dysfunction I have disabled my risk assessment functions. However, it is obvious that you should commence operations immediately."

More wolves, wolves he would certainly have to kill. Elroy already had too much blood on his hands for the sake of Wiggles. Having come this far, he could see little point in turning back. Elroy said a brief prayer for those about to die. He checked the charge on the energy pistol, placed his finger on the firing stud, and palmed open the service hatch.

Welcome Into the Presence of the Lord

Elroy stood before a great pair of double doors. They were carved each from a single brass-bound slab of teak four meters tall, decorated with complex motifs of twining leaves. The grand hall where he stood was littered with the burnt corpses of four security wolves. Part of the carpet was on fire. He mildly regretted the flash burns on the glorious doors. Three different kinds of alarms wailed in the distance.

Elroy raised a spacesuit-clad foot and kicked open the right hand door.

Like the chamber of the Animal's Concilium, the audience chamber of Lord Liasis was transparently roofed. Elroy stepped forward then stopped, his eyes drawn up by a green glare.

There were no stars, no depths of space above him. Instead, a network of greenery rose, curving out in two directions to meet in the sky high over his head, extending unguessably far in its long axis. It had to be at least two or three kilometers to the far side of the green sky. Adrenaline rush of combat forgotten, Elroy stared into the infinite life of plants.

He was accustomed to the riot of the green jungles of Texas, lianas and giant ferns and glossy dark-leaved orchids in the lower reaches, punctuating the echoing silences of the deep forest, while high above in the middle layers and the canopy a violent profusion of epiphytic and parasitic plants hosted butterflies, monkeys, insects, birds and animals of all descriptions. His home tree in Pilot Knob stood amid a roaring chaos of viridian life, changeless in its endless cycle of destruction and renewal.

The Heligan Garden was a different order of nature altogether. Elroy's energy pistol dropped to point toward the carpet as he stared up at roses, ivy, yew, boxwood and a thousand plants for which he had no name. In all their shades and color they grew in glorious array, relieved by paths and walls and smooth rolled meadows, interspersed with pleasaunces and statuary and cunning ponds whose banks had clearly been laid stone by stone at the direction of generations of master craftsmen.

An overpowering scent of green, tame and orderly but powerful, swept through him. Elroy realized Lord Liasis' audience chamber roof was not transparent. It was absent. The room was open to kilometers of the most cultivated garden in existence.

"Just one of my seven gardens. Admittedly, perhaps the finest."

Elroy raised his pistol, turned to look at Lord Liasis. The High Commissioner of the Cis-Lunar Justiciary and Lord of Implementation for the Atlantic Maritime Territories was a thin man, slightly shorter than Elroy's two meters, with flowing white hair. His eyes were a piercing shade of green, and his smile had a natural bonhomie. Clad in a blue morning suit, he carried a glass of wine in his right hand.

Wiggles stood next to Lord Liasis, looking down at his feet and smoothing his flowered green waistcoat with his thumbed paws. Elroy thought Wiggles' tail wagged.

Behind them the audience chamber stretched for several hundred meters, unroofed in glorious green and carpeted in burgundy and gold. There was no furniture save a wooden throne against the distant wall.

"What of the apples of your Lord?" Elroy asked in a soft voice.

"My gardens have many trees." Liasis' smile stretched to a toothsome grin. "Some bear strange fruit."

"And your tale, sir pug?"

Wiggles looked up at Elroy. "True, as far as it went. Not the entire truth."

Elroy stroked the trigger of the energy pistol. The vest whispered risks and priorities in his ear, but he ignored it. "What would be the entire truth?"

Liasis' smile dropped away as he spoke, his voice mild and his tone almost bemused. "One legacy of the La Grangian restoration is a strong prohibition against hereditary power. The Secretaries-General taught them that lesson. When a man ascends to a position of great responsibilities, there is a certain, ah, physical price that must be paid."

"Some do cheat," Wiggles added, "but it is frowned upon. There are no children, normally."

"I have need of a young man, a human, of compassion and strength, wit and ruthlessness. I have strong preference that he not spring from the Great Families of the high places, so as to be free of our politics and alliances. Lord Deimos offered a younger nephew, but the eventual price would have been far too high."

"My home is in a tree in the jungles of Texas, with the family I hope to establish. I have no wish to meddle in the business of the Lords of the High Places."

Liasis gestured with the wine glass. "Would you care for some? From Scandinavia's finest vineyards. Orbital wine is never quite the same, you know."

"Elroy." Wiggles' voice was earnest. "Let me be plain. I was sent to travel among the people of Earth, to find and test a worthy successor from outside the circles of the ruling classes. I required a young man who would bring no untoward ambition with him into the Gardens of Sweet Night. You are the one success I encountered—capable, thoughtful, ethical and strong. At my recommendation, and on the strength of your journey here, Lord Liasis now seeks you for his heir, to train and mentor that you might someday become a Lord of space."

Elroy shook his head. "What a strange way to choose an heir. Had you asked me to come here and be a gardener, I might have rejoiced." He laid the pistol down on the carpet, careful to point it away from the Lord Liasis and his chancellor.

"Had you brought me here and shown me the curve of the blue Earth and your wondrous Gardens, offering me dominion in exchange for loyalty freely given, I might have rejoiced.

"Instead, at your behest, I have beaten, wounded and killed, staining my soul with blood. I made an Animal into a beast. Four wolves lie dead outside your very door, other men and Animals maimed and wounded along the way. My vows are broken, lives have been ruined or taken, all for your little game." Elroy dropped the vest to the carpet.

Lord Liasis' voice was gentle. "No. Not for a game. For dominion over the kingdoms of the Earth and the high places. A small price to pay for proof of your fitness to succeed me. We test those outside the pale because it is the only true way to find new blood."

Elroy began to strip off the silver space suit. "Lord, in taking service with Chancellor Wiggles, I sold my freedom and made choices to do things I regret. Acting on my own I would not so much as kill a man to take an apple from him. Why would I kill for something as foolish as dominion over the kingdoms of the Earth? All I ever wanted was to start a family — the very thing you would deny me even with all your proffered riches."

Elroy dropped the space suit, then tossed the purser's coat onto the carpet, followed by Nero's knife and his carefully hoarded pay. He turned to walk away, stopping before the door to look back at Liasis and Wiggles once more.

"The world, Elroy," whispered Liasis, spreading an open hand. "I can give you the world, and these gardens in the sky. What greater gift is there?"

"Lord Liasis, dominion is a hard sentence to serve. My greater gift to myself is that I choose to remain free. I leave your service as I entered it."

"Many wolves wait outside," said Wiggles. The pug's tone was both hopeful and sad.

"I know." Elroy looked up one last time at the Heligan Garden, breathed in the peaceful scent of green, then opened the door to walk out free and unafraid.

author's afterword

Deborah Layne, publisher and editor of Wheatland Press, has played a large role in my career since before I even had one. She has been friend, confidante, cheerleader, marketing guru *par excellence*, and above all she has kept me honest.

American Sorrows was Deborah's idea. I'd been grumbling about the difficulties of marketing a novella I quite liked, and she pointed out that there had been increasing interest of late in longer works by various authors in the field. So we noodled tables of contents for a collection of novelettes and novellas to be built around my Hugo-nominated novelette, "Into the Gardens of Sweet Night."

A little while later, through the intestinal magic of publishing, the excellent James Van Pelt produced a kind introduction, Aynjel Kaye supplied a stunning cover photo, and the good people at Scorpius Digital agreed to do a simultaneous e-book release—a first for both Wheatland Press and for me.

"Our Lady of American Sorrows"

This story literally came to me in a dream, or at least the first scene did. I was on a flat-topped roof in a dusty Central American town with my best friend—we were both in high school—watching a convoy of red Chevy Suburbans roll by, filled with priests. It was utterly clear to me, in that way that dream knowledge can be, that these big, burly men with their hard, narrow eyes and their dog collars were French *Legionnaires Étrangeres*, come to do mischief in my town.

I woke with that image dense in my head and wondered what they were about. The rest flowed from the keyboard, surprising me as most of my stories do.

There's a discussion that all writers get in to from time to time, a variation on "what exactly did you mean by thus-and-such." If I could answer that question, I'd be teaching contemporary lit somewhere. All I do is write them. Interpretation is an exercise for the reader.

But I look at a story like "Our Lady of American Sorrows" and I see echoes of many things. My childhood in Asia and Africa, transmuted to the boy Peter in this other version of Central America. Edd O'Donnell's Chevy Surburban, years ago back in Austin, Texas, though it was white rather than red. The Orthodox monasteries of Bulgaria I visited in my late teens. My long fascination with the very concept of an anti-pope, and eventually learning some of the history of the Avignon Papacy which infuses the backstory of this piece.

All this probably means something. What, I don't know. But New Albion was an interesting place to visit, though I wouldn't want to live there. If I could, I'd walk Water Avenue out to the monastery, just to see that cliff wall over the river. I'd explore the *sacbe*, hoping to meet who Peter and Rodger met there.

"Daddy's Caliban"

Oddly enough—for I would generally say this isn't true of me— "Daddy's Caliban" also came to me in a dream, not unlike "Our Lady of American Sorrows." I'd been thinking about the Lord of the Rings, specifically the old towers Tolkein mentions in the Westmarch, at the edge of the Shire. As a child I'd always been fascinated by that, and longed for ancient Elven architecture at the far end of whatever street we lived on that year. (Never mind that I was living in Taiwan or Nigeria or Bulgaria, and whatever we had at the end of the street that year was a lot more interesting in real life than Elven towers—it is the nature of people to want most what they do not have.)

One night I dreamt of an ordinary suburban subdivision, the kind I've never lived in but which could be found anywhere from Long Island to Long Beach, with an ancient Elven tower standing in a field at the edge of the housing with an electric blue glow in its old stones. In my dream, adults paid this no more mind than they paid the neighborhood fire hydrants, but the children were fascinated.

So I sat down a day or two later and allowed my fingers to wonder what it would mean to have such a thing in your world, and to have such a thing be ordinary, or at least familiar.

All fiction is somewhat autobiographical. Henry and Cameron live in a house pretty much where my house is located in Portland, Oregon, behind a bluff next to a north-flowing river, though their house is much smaller than mine. The town is a miniature version of Lowell, Massachusetts, where I have family. Is it American enough to be in *American Sorrows*? I can't say. The geography is, and I think the sensibility is, though I recognize that the conceits are Old World, not New World.

One final note on the Old World. I must extend my deepest thanks to editor/publisher Andy Cox of TTA Press in the United Kingdom, and his excellent magazine *The Third Alternative*. Some time ago Andy was kind enough to accept "Daddy's Caliban" for a September, 2004 publication date in *The Third Alternative*. When Deborah Layne and I set about putting *American Sorrows* together, I very much wanted to include "Daddy's Caliban" here as a reprint. Unfortunately, this book's publication date is also September, 2004. Andy was kind enough to grant me permission to do this, with *The Third Alternative* as the first appearance of record regardless of what may come in printing or shipping delays. As in so many other matters over the past few years, Andy has been very supportive of me in this.

"The River Knows Its Own"

This story is a companion piece to an upcoming *Asimov's* story called "Dark Flowers, Inverse Moon." Both are novelette-length explorations of aspects of magic in the contemporary world, certainly territory that does not lack for coverage in our genre.

What I like about both these stories, and what I hope might set them apart from their profusion of similars, is a sense of place that was almost overwhelming to me when I wrote them. "Dark Flowers" is set in Central Texas, where I lived for eighteen years. "The River Knows Its Own" is set in the area in and around Portland, Oregon, where I have lived since 2000.

The issue for me in writing about magic, any magic, is believability. As a reader, I'm capable of consuming high fantasy by the barrelload, but when I sit down to write inside a magic system, I get bogged down in the inherent improbabilities. Magic, as satisfying as it is as a literary trope, seems inherently silly to me. There is rarely if ever an accounting of the costs of it, let alone any recognition of conservation of mass, energy or momentum — the realities of life which even dragons and wizards must endure, assuming their are not immune to gravity or the effects of mass.

So in order for me to work with magic, the rest of the story has to be tied down very tightly, anchored to something firm. Hence, "The River Knows Its Own", set in around the place where I live my daily life. In the end, I suppose it's easier for me to believe in dragons winging over Portland than it is for me to believe in dragons winging over High Serhuna.

"Into the Gardens of Sweet Night"

Several years ago Bruce Holland Rogers came to a meeting of Wordos, the writers' group of which I am a member, and asked for submissions to *Bones of the World*, an anthology he was editing for Jeffry Dwight at SFF.Net Press. He was trying to finish the book out, and wasn't quite happy with all of his slush.

So I went off and wrote a story called "The Courtesy of Guests," which was in the due course of time accepted by Bruce, and published in the book. Page 365, if you're wondering. And I didn't have to look that up. It was my first sale, and my first publication.

But while I was waiting for Bruce to tell me whether or not he would take the story, I was moved to write another piece to the same guidelines. That was "Into the Gardens of Sweet Night." Since Bruce bought "The Courtesy of Guests", "Gardens" made the other rounds, being rejected by the finest of markets. It's a bit long for a first story from a new author, it rambles, it commits a dozen literary sins of which I am not even yet aware.

Fast forward to the second half of 2002. The kind people who run *L. Ron Hubbard's Writers of the Future Contest* sent me an email telling me that I was no longer eligible to enter, as I had sold too much work. (I had been entering assiduously for a while.) I wrote back and thanked them, and asked permission to enter one last time. When they acceded, I sent "Into the Gardens of Sweet Night."

The story took first place in the third quarter of contest year XIX. Big excitement. Trip to L.A. Terrific workshop with Tim Powers, K.D. Wentworth, a cast of dozens. Giant awards ceremony replete with tuxes, celebrities and speeches. Big fat trophy, big fat check. Happy happy joy joy.

"Into the Gardens of Sweet Night" then went on to be a Hugo nominee for Best Novelette. As of this writing, the votes are still being sent in. I have modest expectations and high excitement of the future, but consider this:

It's the first Writers of the Future story to ever make the Hugo ballot.

This story made the Hugo ballot almost three years to the day after I received my very first acceptance for "The Courtesy of Guests."

So even when I go to Boston and cheer for Michael Swanwick or Jeffrey Ford or whoever walks off with *my* golden rocket, I'm going to be proud of that story in a way which I will never forget.

And by God do I owe Bruce Holland Rogers a debt of gratitude, or at a minimum a glass of wine.

Jay Lake
Portland, Oregon
July, 2004

OTHER TITLES AVAILABLE FROM

WHEATLAND PRESS

ANTHOLOGIES

POLYPHONY 1, Deborah Layne and Jay Lake, Eds. Volume one in the critically acclaimed slipstream/cross-genre series will feature stories from Maureen McHugh, Andy Duncan, Carol Emshwiller, Lucius Shepard and others.

POLYPHONY 2, Deborah Layne and Jay Lake, Eds. Volume two in the critically acclaimed slipstream/cross-genre series will feature stories from Alex Irvine, Theodora Goss, Jack Dann, Michael Bishop and others.

POLYPHONY 3, Deborah Layne and Jay Lake, Eds. Volume three in the critically acclaimed slipstream/cross-genre series will feature stories from Jeff Ford, Bruce Holland Rogers, Ray Vukcevich, Robert Freeman Wexler and others.

POLYPHONY 4, Deborah Layne and Jay Lake, Eds. Volume four in the critically acclaimed slipstream/cross-genre series will feature stories from Jeff VanderMeer, Stepan Chapman, Alex Irvine, Kit Reed, Don Webb, Gavin Grant and others.

TEL: STORIES, Jay Lake Ed. An anthology of experimental fiction with authors to be announced.

EXQUISITE CORPUSCLE, Frank Wu and Jay Lake Eds. Stories, poems, illustrations, even a play; an elaborate game of literary telephone featuring Gary Shockley, Benjamin Rosenbaum, Bruce Holland Rogers, Kristin Livdahl, Maggie Hogarth, and others.

ALL STAR ZEPPELIN ADVENTURE STORIES, David Moles and Jay Lake Eds. Original zeppelin stories by Jim Van Pelt, Leslie What, and others; one reprint, "You Could Go Home Again" by Howard Waldrop.

SINGLE-AUTHOR COLLECTIONS

DREAM FACTORIES AND RADIO PICTURES, Howard Waldrop. Waldrop's stories about early film and television reprinted in one volume.

GREETINGS FROM LAKE WU, Jay Lake and Frank Wu. Collection of stories by Jay Lake with original illustrations by Frank Wu.

TWENTY QUESTIONS, Jerry Oltion. Twenty brilliant works by the Nebula Award-winning author of "Abandon in Place."

THE BEASTS OF LOVE, Steven Utley, Intro. by Lisa Tuttle. Utley's "love" stories spanning the past twenty years; a brilliant mixture of science fiction, fantasy and horror.

NONFICTION

WEAPONS OF MASS SEDUCTION, Lucius Shepard. A collection of Shepard's film reviews. Some have previously appeared in print in the *Magazine of Fantasy and Science Fiction*; most have only appeared online at *Electric Story*.

POETRY

KNUCKLE SANDWICHES, Tom Smario, Intro. by Lucius Shepard. Poems about boxing by a long-time poet and cut-man.

NOVEL

PARADISE PASSED, Jerry Oltion. The crew of a colony ship must choose between a ready-made paradise and one they create for themselves.

FOR ORDERING INFORMATION VISIT:
WWW.WHEATLANDPRESS.COM

Printed in the United States
44098LVS00004B/334-366